Help Me, Jacques Cousteau

Gil Adamson

Gil A[damson] (signature)

The Porcupine's Quill

. . . .

CANADIAN CATALOGUING
IN PUBLICATION DATA

Adamson, Gil
    Help me, Jacques Cousteau

ISBN 0-88984-161-6

I. Title.

PS8551.D35H4 1995 C813'.54 C95-931794-5
PR9199.3.A43H4 1995

Published by The Porcupine's Quill, Inc., 68 Main
Street, Erin, Ontario NOB 1TO with financial
assistance from The Canada Council and the
Ontario Arts Council. The support of the
Government of Ontario through the Ministry of
Culture, Tourism and Recreation is also
gratefully acknowledged, as is the support of the
Department of Canadian Heritage through the
Book and Periodical Industry Development
Programme and the Periodical Distribution
Assistance Programme.

Represented in Canada by the Literary Press
Group. Trade orders are available from General
Distribution Services.

Readied for the press by John Metcalf.
Copy edited by Doris Cowan.

Cover is after a photograph by Adrian Adamson.

Contents

ERIC SCHLOSS, M.D., FRCPC
Diseases of the Skin
#504 Hys Centre, 11010 - 101 Street N.W.
Edmonton, Alberta T5H 4B9
Telephone (780) 432-0803 Fax (780) 439-4642

Date ....

Patient's Name ....

Address ....

PHN# __ __ __ __ __ / __ __ __ __

Refill Instructions	0	1	2	3	4		NR

℞

14/1995

*signed by author

Dr. Signature _____

Heaven is a place where nothing ever happens.

– Talking Heads

The Lakemba

I SEE THE LONG HEAVY sofa come skating
across the linoleum and I step out of its path. The
sky outside the window is grey and most of the
people in the lounge are green. The sofa collides
with the wall, seems to consider the situation a
moment, then heads out over the floor again. My
mother looks up from where she sits, her cheeks
a flaming red, a lamp tilting solicitously above
her head.

She sees that I'm okay and goes back to her
book: *The Alexandria Quartet*. In her mind, a
mighty library is burning, vellum pages float out
the windows and are carried on the breeze out to
sea. My mother is in love with Balthazar. The
lamp above her swings to lean over the woman
next to her, as if to see what this one's reading. I
see the sofa coming again. A plastic duck on
wheels drifts into its path and, with a muffled
squeak, it is creamed against the wall.

We're on our way home from Australia in a
boat called the *Lakemba*, and soon we will cross
the equator. Sun glares on the wide deck. Wooden
tanning chairs have been strapped down and the
sea rises and sinks at an angle to the deck that is

. . . .

woozy and keeps changing. I sit on a plastic horse
and lift my feet. I drift over the floor toward my
mother. Her face comes up, flushed and young
and voracious for Balthazar. She looks up. 'Oh,
darling!' she says and extends a thin hand to me,
but I drift away again, tables, chairs, other
children, the eight-foot sofa, all of it moving in
sluggish orbits.

'Are you hot? It's so hot,' she says, blinking.

'Come back,' she says, and we both wait for it
to happen.

They tell us it can get a lot worse. But today is
the fourth bad day and anyway, I'm getting used
to it. My mother's worried about me, not having
any other kids to worry about yet. But I'm all
right. All I dread is going to bed, the moonless
night and the wild, moving wall by my bed.

* * *

It's night and we're eight days away from
Vancouver, the ship still lost in the dark and
nothing anywhere to show us that this is not a
dream. Above the upper decks, festooned with
small lights and nosing into the night, are masts
and antennae and other strange lines and pipes
and funnels. The lights chart the shape of the
boat. The white floors of the decks appear to be
an empty stage with spotlights shining down.
The occasional woman totters by, the occasional
boy in a wrinkled white uniform. At midnight,
the captain marches past with a woman clinging
to each arm. He walks a perfect line, as if
magnetically attached to the pitching metal floor.
My mother, unable to sleep, peers from the
window of our cabin and sees the threesome pass
by – a man with two female flags, waving in the
night wind.

The Lakemba

'There they are again, North!' she whispers to my father, who sleeps on, 'How can they drink in this heat?' Then she comes and looks at me where I lie like a wiener in a bun, a rolled blanket on either side of the bunk and my body wedged between them.

Night time is a horror to me on this ship. I am so young that I forget that every day ends with me going to bed. I sleep in the top bunk. The steel feet are riveted to the floor, but not securely enough, so that with every lurch of the ship, my bed leaves the wall and yawns out into the dark room. I try, absurdly, to hold on to a flat wall with my damp fingers. The bed dangles on the precipice, decides not to topple over this time, and sails back with a sharp *whang* against the wall. This process is repeated, unrelenting, until I fall asleep. I dream of our apartment in Sydney, the houses next door, and the whole cardboard cluster of our neighbourhood, all knocking heads and rattling like goods on a truck.

In case of evacuation, my mother has packed an emergency kit: Band-Aids, rubbing alcohol, scissors, stomach remedies, a small mouldy package of cookies, a knife, baby aspirin, a crossword book. We are heading for the equator in a headlong rush, as if to get the suspense over with and start roasting. The engines roar and throb through the metal framework of the ship. My mother, her forehead damp with sweat, is staring at the black heaving water, the deep valley and peak, and close in the wake of the ship, the ornamental curl of white. She is standing on the deck at sunset, without a thought in her head, the emergency kit in her limp grasp, while behind her, through the open lounge door, come the sounds and moving shadows of a movie. People wander around the deck in silence and pass on down the metal stairwells. Someone is screaming with laughter somewhere, but, to my mother, it is the caw of a bird. The purser staggers by, his sleeves rolled up.

'Excuse me!' my mother starts, but he is gone into the bowl of the setting sun, a shadow-puppet jiggled before a roaring fire.

My father has been teaching in Australia; an offer to teach one term in Canadian studies somehow stretched to two years. He's been fighting his way through the halls of a high school in Sydney, pulling maps down from the ceiling and poking holes in them with a pointer, reading poetry out loud, singing with the woeful choir, and exchanging blistering wisecracks with other teachers. Not being one of them, he's looked on as a kind of intelligent ape. After all, where he comes from, water circles the drain the wrong way.

My father has committed to memory folk songs, sayings, long heroic mining poems involving dogs and dynamite. He believes, privately, that marsupials are a perversion of nature. He has listened to the red desert hulk of Ayers Rock hissing in the rain, an occurrence so rare that, when he told his colleagues about it, he was not believed. He has ventured into the outback with bored guides and my mother swooning beside him in the jeep, eaten cooked snake, lain awake in the dark and heard the chuckle of night birds. He has heard the low creepy growl of the didgeridoo and the bird-like flutter of the bull-roar. He has perfected his mimicry of the accent. He has laughed out loud in restaurants and lunchrooms and barber shops and banks at things that no one else considered funny. He stood in the cool wind of Sydney harbour with the gulls overhead and stared at the green streaks along the hull of the ship he must eventually board to return to Canada, and he wondered what else in his future could possibly equal this.

We are passing over the equator. Heat stroke is general on the ship. We are like John Glenn, burning through the atmosphere, falling to earth. The lights on the mast spark and flicker at night, rivets in the metal walls and flooring seem loose. No one moves on the decks anymore during the day. Cabin doors are left open with the vague shapes of reclined figures within. Everywhere is the rising and subsiding buzz of the engines, the stairwells clamorous, the lounge empty, and even the glorified mess hall unoccupied, except for a couple of drunken teens, and a dog flat under a table. In this blazing cemetery, while Dad lies dreaming, my mother rises like a sodden ghost from the bed and staggers, furious, out of the cabin.

'Excuse me!' she says to an empty deck, 'Somebody?'

According to my mother's telling of it, the captain was entertaining when she burst in. He had the two women there, who had been engaged in a complex and private business with him since three days out. They sat playing cards in their underclothes. My mother had her emergency kit with her and she shook it menacingly at him.

'I've been to the purser, or bursar, or whatever you call the stupid man! And I've been to the

engineer! They keep sending me to someone
else.'

'Madame ...'

'I have children to look after!' she said,
forgetting for the moment that she only had one
child.

'Madame ...' the captain said, rising and
wiping his palm before offering it to my mother.
She paid no attention to his hand or his grey
underwear or to the room she was in, but carried
on as if run by batteries.

'I've tried to get that idiot man in E12 to come
out and help me. I have a child that's burning up.
And now I'm forced to come here. This is the
most shoddy, maddening ship I've ever been on!'
She said this as if she had made a career of being
on ships. The two women had somehow
disappeared into the murk of the huge apartment,
perhaps into a closet or a bedroom or a toilet.
They were just gone, as if vaporized. My mother
blinked.

'Madame,' tried the captain again, 'how can I
help you?' She looked at him, her face slick with
sweat.

'If I don't get a fan in my cabin in four minutes
I'm moving my mattress onto the deck!'

* * *

The fan rattled away, freshly bolted to the metal
wall. I stood at my mother's side, blocking the
breeze, and poked her in the ear. She brushed me
away. I leaned over and stared with one of my
eyes into the dark brown pool of one of hers.

'You're sweaty,' I said and she groaned. She
was lying on the unmade bed, one leg hanging off,
when my father appeared at the door with the
doctor. As it turned out, my mother had

dysentery and was running a temperature of 104.

'Oh,' she said, 'that's why I'm seeing those things,' gesturing at nothing.

* * *

It's Christmas dinner on the equator, sliding down the leeward side in a luxuriant easing off of heat. We're heading north, heading home, in a happy rocking nausea, and all day the smells issuing from the kitchen have been assailing my parents with memories. For my part, I have never seen snow. I learned to speak the language in Sydney, Australia, and inexplicably all of my friends have Canadian accents. They say 'Hi' instead of 'G'day.' My father asks me what I want for Christmas, which is strange, because it's not like he can go out and buy it, and also because what I ask for is a beach ball.

In my future there is no beach ball. Instead, there is a plastic sheet that works like a toboggan. And a torturous, unbending snowsuit – a whole world of children waddling around in torturous unbending snowsuits. A world of sleds and snow and slush and ice-balls down the back of my neck and soggy knees and the maddening zzt-zzt of nylon snow pants; the throttle of wool scarves, yanked tight by my mother and impossible to claw open; the stink of cloakrooms; the multi-coloured Popsicle look of cold feet and the shrieking pangs while they thaw; the blue-grey, motionless mornings where the backyard is erased by snow, where airborne debris lands, punctures the lunar surface, sinks out of sight. I have winter ahead of me, and I ask for a beach ball.

My mother is feeling better now, hiding in the
cabin in case a bursar or purser should walk past,
or in case the captain in his nocturnal wanderings
should pass by with his women. But there is no
one on the decks except the long, flat dog who
slinks under tanning chairs and licks the painted
metal floor for crumbs and spilled sweet drinks. I
follow him and pat the stiff hair on his back and
he ignores me. Together we cover the ship in a
thorough and efficient manner, checking all
corners and speeding past certain doorways
where, perhaps, there is an angry kicked shoe or a
flung book.

In this way I see people I have never seen
before. Women with brown legs snapping their
bathing suits beside the tiny, boxy swimming
pool. Small men sweating in rooms that clang
with pipes and meters and valves. Kitchen boys
who steal above to stand on deck and let the cool
air rush through their clothes, to smoke and talk
together and flick the glowing butts out into the
ocean.

I follow my dog until Mum arrives, furious
with panic, having searched and searched and fled
in her mind from the certainty that I had slipped
under a guard-rail and drowned. On wobbly legs,
she carries me down to dinner where we sit with
strangers, our water glasses illustrating the
concept of level, gravy searching the perimeter of
our plates for a way out.

Outside, the lifeboats rock in their steel
hammocks, the canvas tarps that cover them
undulating in the cooling breeze. The *Lakemba*
chugs onward into the sparkling Pacific. Three
years from this date, in the early hours of the

morning, this ship will sink whole into the ocean, and these lifeboats will groan under the weight of panicking, sun-sick passengers. My mother will not be there to use her emergency kit containing scissors, cookies, baby aspirin. My father will be driving through the snow to work, singing out loud in his frost-dull car, perhaps wondering what the weather is like in Sydney, in the harbour, where the ships stand high in the water and the cranes swing all day and all night, carrying things away.

As for me, I will be enrolled in school and pondering daily a way to get sick or go truant or just get kicked out. A dog will be my only entertainment. I will be throwing biscuits out into the snow for the dog and locking him out and laughing when he comes back and hangs his head and drools the gummy pieces on the step, abusing me till I let him in again, wagging and snapping and soaking the floor with snow.

Fear Itself

MY UNCLE CASTOR IS RICH. He lives in a very large stone house which stands by itself near the lake and is surrounded by tall spruce trees full of crows. He has a fondness for animals and so, over the years, he has acquired dogs, cats, pigeons, geese, a rabbit, and a horse. All his collected animals are pure white. His main irritation now is that he has acquired a second rabbit. He stands in the middle of the lawn and looks at this new rabbit, points at it and says, 'What the *hell* am I supposed to do with this?' It is mud-brown. It is also a very happy rabbit, apparently, and it spreads out on the grass, with its hind legs stretched back, and goes to sleep. My uncle storms away.

We come to visit in the summer, bring news about other members of the family, fight all the way in the car about whether Dad should turn the car around and avoid this year's travesty. As usual, we arrive smiling, the adults tense and towering around me. I ignore them all and run across a seemingly endless lawn, hop across the stony beach, and leap into the lake.

Just after Aunt Netty left him, Castor voiced his opinion that dogs are better than family. I think he meant that a dog will love you under any circumstances, no matter how much of a bastard you are, and it will die first. Both of these things are a problem for my uncle. Not that he makes it easy for anyone close to him to love him. My father, Castor and the third brother, Bishop, were sent off to boarding school together. Once there, Castor was free to exercise his power; he was larger, more forceful than the other boys, and he had a knack for not getting caught. My father found cover in the library and studied geology, weather patterns, natural disasters. Bishop, armoured by a mute hostility to everything expected of him, finally escaped Castor by joining the cadets and, later, the navy. In that school, at that age, my father says, Castor was fear itself. And now, alone in this house, with Netty gone, he's almost worse.

There is a blow-up at night. I wake up to the sound of shouting and I blink at the dark light bulb on my ceiling. I can hear the lake too and, closer to the house, something moving out on the lawn, perhaps a dog, nose down, hunting. I jump at the sound of a door slamming, and a moment later there is the sound of my mother laughing. It's a laugh of exasperation.

In the morning, there is a game, to cheer everyone up. We stand on the concrete pier as Castor takes the cat, the dog, and the goose out in the row boat. He tows the horse behind by a halter. The object of the game is to see which reaches land first – my mother makes vague objections, but she's just as curious as the rest of

us. We watch as he lets all the animals go at once.
Of course, it's the cat that wins, clinging to
Castor at first, cutting and scratching him until
he is compelled to fling it violently into the
water. Droop-eared and furious, it tries to get
back into the boat until shoved away with an oar.
All this time wasted fighting the inevitable, and
the cat still makes it back to shore first. It humps
past us up the concrete steps, looking half its
usual size, and streaks across the lawn to lie
under a bush and hate us.

My mother takes me to the back of the house
where the garden is full-blown and wild and gone
to seed. It has been that way since Netty left, 'fed
to the teeth with his nonsense', as my mother
puts it. Still the roses and the vines seem to keep
to the dark line of the soil, never crossing over to
the lawn, and everywhere there is the hum of
insects. We sit and eat lemon cake which my
mother has baked. She sits cross-legged with me
in silence. We put a piece of cake out on the grass
and watch as ants cover it. My mother and I share
a fondness for watching insects from a safe
distance.

Days and nights drift into each other,
punctuated by dinner, lunch, trips to town.
Sometimes I hear roaring fights at night,
sometimes either my father or Castor roaring
with laughter. One evening after dinner I get into
my bathing suit and Castor and I go to the pool,
which is big and concrete and shaped like an
eight. There are leaves on the surface and the
bottom is black with debris, but the water is clear
enough. It is getting quite dark so my uncle
disappears into the pump room and after a second
the lights in the sides of the pool snap on. There

is a loud hum. He comes out again, fighting his
way through the bushes, cursing.

'Hope there isn't a short circuit,' he says and I
pause on the pulpy diving board and look at him.
I back away, wondering out loud if we should
poke it with a stick or a rubber boot or something
first.

'Only way to tell,' he says smiling, 'is to jump
in.' I realize I've made a crucial error getting up
on the board first, and start to quail. But Castor
gives me that look, the black eyeball, and I run
and jump, no hesitation. Up into the night air,
then down and under the bright, glittering water,
my arms ahead of me like a blind person. There's
no shock, not that I can tell, so I open my eyes. I
can see all the hairs on my arm. I watch them
wave back and forth as the bulk of Castor hits the
surface after me.

'You know what it's like?' my father says. 'You
go into your room and there are clothes on your
bed from grade seven, laid out for you to put on.
You're supposed to get into them and walk
around like a fool.' I frown at my father, waiting
for him to explain all that. He fiddles with his
belt buckle.

'That's what it's like to come here,' he says.

The two of them go out in the early morning,
Dad and Uncle Castor. They walk into the woods
with rifles. While they are gone animals rush out
from the trees, a skunk, a deer, the brown rabbit.
They stop on the gravel driveway and pant. After
a while they make their slow way back into the
dark woods. Later my uncle emerges with my
father following. They say they didn't find
anything, that they just sat on a large rock and

discussed my father's future. By the way my father is standing, the wild look in his eyes, I guess that it's true. But later a neighbour comes round and says his dog was grazed by a bullet. He is chased away by Castor who follows him halfway down the lane. The rabbit hops slowly after them both, looking for attention.

My mother figures in all of this too, being under constant pressure to cook. Aunt Netty, whose name he will not allow spoken, is gone, so some woman must cook. My mother flatly refuses to cook for him and we three sit down to a meal while he rages around the house, cursing. Sometimes he points at the rifle and threatens to shoot me. I keep my head down, keep eating. My mother acts like she doesn't even hear him, like he doesn't exist. Eventually he gives up and makes himself some soup and comes to sit with us, slurping loudly, as if nothing happened.

My mother pours me a bath. She says: 'He just wants people to know he's alive, that's all.'
'I know he's alive.'
'Everyone's the same. Everyone wants things to go their way.'
She leaves me alone in the wide cold bathroom, vines coming in the window, small black and white tiles on the floor and steam coming up everywhere. I decide that I, too, want things to go my way, but I will never treat my children like Castor treats my dad. I don't know it, yet, but I have a little brother on the way, and despite my good intentions, I will torment him and enjoy it.

One night they turn the stereo on and let all the lights in the house burn. My mother and my

father dance out on the grass in their bathing
suits and Castor sits on the stone steps and
watches, flicks pebbles at them. I am upstairs in
the hallway looking out and I see Castor
disappear into the dark, followed by a dog. When
he's gone, my mother does a strange little dance,
like a belly dance, and then my father leaps and
twirls around. They are laughing, dancing to
please each other. Then the huge shape of a white
goose heaves past them, like a newspaper in the
wind, followed by another and finally the dog and
Castor. I stare down. They're all going crazy down
there on the green lawn.

My mother is physically fantastic. Perhaps
that is what attracted Dad. She's long, tall,
elastic. She can put her feet behind her neck. She
can lie on her stomach, arch her back and make a
perfect u. Measured from fingertip to fingertip
she must be six feet. Sometimes, she would wrap
her thighs about Dad and squeeze until he
panicked and begged and struggled, like Faye
Wray squished between the fingers of King Kong.
When she cuddled him close to her and acted
nice, he went almost crazy with desire. I suppose
these are things a daughter shouldn't know. But I
have my own unusual abilities, and can hear a
conversation through three walls. After years of
listening, I formed an odd portrait of my parents,
and, at that moment in their lives it may have
been a good likeness.

Two evenings later, I had my nightmare. I had
been given some *crème de menthe*, which looks
and smells like candy, but burns like fire. I
whined for a glass until my father, who was
getting drunk, gave me one. It was a calm happy
night and my uncle was pulling books down from

the shelves, excited, trying to prove some point.
My father was saying 'God, no!' and rubbing his
face, but he looked sleepy and content, and
Castor kept saying 'This is it, North, this is what
I mean!'

I sat and stared out the window onto the dark
grass and drank my liquor. Castor was reading
something out loud, bawling the Latin parts in a
leisured way, and my mother was twitching to
get out of the room. In three sips, my drink was
gone and I went to bed pouty and uncomfortable.
'Think about nice things,' my mother
suggested. But I didn't. I thought about where my
Aunt Netty was, lost maybe, out in the night.

In my dream the white horse had got loose
from his stall and kicked at the barn door until it
splintered and fell aside. He clopped out onto the
road and stood waiting, pale neck bowed. I held
my breath and watched helplessly as he lifted his
head and saw me by the barn where I was hiding.
As he approached, his eyes rolled back and stared
white at nothing. I woke with a jolt and heard, in
a far room, the sound of a man crying.

My mother sat on the grass with her legs out
in front and her elbows between them on the
grass. She looked up from the paper.
'Seventeen people fell off a ferry into the
freezing water near Baffin Island, and they all
lived.' My uncle noticed the position she was in.
He stared at her for a long time.
'That is *not* natural!' he burst out finally. My
mother looked up. 'Natural?' she said, 'I'd call it
good luck.'

I crept behind the house and stood looking at

the garden, the brown leaves of the roses, the long bald stems and heavy pink and yellow heads. The summer was getting on and I was trying not to think about school which loomed like a permanent seat at the dentist's. A bumblebee hummed through the roses, struggled from head to head, then rose up and dragged itself to the next bush. I noticed another bumblebee to the left, and then another and then more. The wind died and I could hear them all. For a second I saw everything alive and moving at once. I can't help liking things like that. I had a teacher at school called Mrs Vittie who liked to throw things. She'd act patient for a while, then suddenly turn blood red, lose her cool and throw something. One time she threw two chalk brushes, her shoes, books. Kids were shrieking and ducking. One moment the class was frozen, waiting for it to happen, and then everything started moving at once.

It was the day before we were to leave. My father had been in the basement rewiring the house. He told me he could never relax in his brother's house and so he had to find things to do. It pleased him to change things, so switches in one place were attached to light bulbs in another. The pool lights were connected to the kitchen. The hall light was in the one spare bedroom. As of last year, the bathroom light was somehow disconnected entirely so we all had to go in the dark. I have never been scared in the dark because I can hear anything moving around, no matter how small it is. I know when I'm not alone. But my mother suffered. At night she would always take the dog. She called it the outhouse, even though it was indoors.

My Uncle Castor began looking at us in a

· ·

funny way. He got sullen. I figured he was
beginning to miss us, even though we hadn't gone
yet, and if you asked him, he'd probably say we
were freeloaders, good riddance. He stood out by
the barn and fed the horse, brushed it and dug dirt
from its hooves. He took the dog to the lake and
washed it and threw sticks for it into the water.
The dog crashed into the water until all the soap
had rinsed off. He seemed to be taking stock of
his animals. The horse, dogs, cats, rabbits. The
geese and pigeons he didn't care about too much,
but he went and looked at them, just looked. He
bent over a goose which stood on the lawn and
goggled up at him. He shuffled his feet and it
backed away. He stared at the spot where it had
been.

The morning we were supposed to leave, I
came down to the kitchen and looked out the
window which ran the length of the counter. It
was a wet morning and mist poured out of the
trees onto the gravel driveway. My stomach
growled. After a minute I saw my Aunt Netty
standing at the edge of the woods with her hands
on her hips. It looked like she'd stepped out of the
trees. She looked up at the house for a while, then
walked briskly up the stone steps and through the
door. A little later I heard Castor howling to my
father, pounding on his bedroom door like it was
Christmas day.

I searched the fridge for something easy to eat,
then got excited about cooking something.
Perhaps I could make breakfast for Netty and my
parents. I had never seen anyone cook for Castor,
and so the idea was alien to me. I took out the
skillet and burned two eggs to black crusts before
my mother came rushing down and took the pan

from me. Her long arms stuck out of the sleeves of her housecoat as if she had grown during the night.

'She came home,' I said and my mother laughed.

'She certainly did.'

'Would you ever leave Dad?' I asked wondering if this could happen to me, my mother walking off into the woods, or rowing over the lake.

'There are things that could make me; I won't lie to you about it. There's something about men and marriage that I don't like.' She stood there for a second, thinking.

'No,' she said and put a plate of eggs down in front of me, 'your uncle and aunt are a whole different case. Don't judge the world based on them.'

I hadn't expected all of that. I just wanted her to say 'No.'

A spot of light fell through the tree above and drifted over the plate of cookies, and I watched it, waiting till everything was set and we could begin. We'd decided to stay until evening. After all, this was historic; the first tea on the lawn since Netty had been gone. In some ways it seemed she'd never left. Already there was a pile of brambles and dead branches at one end of the lawn and several broken aluminum chairs were tossed on top. Both bathrooms had been boiled and scrubbed, and the fridge stood open, defrosting.

Later I sat in my bathing suit on the grass and ate cookies. For once my mother hadn't made me wait half an hour before I could eat, which she usually did out of fear I would die of cramps.

· ·

Netty came across the lawn with a plate and
Castor sat back, watching her come, and sighed.
She was dressed in a long blue sari with gold
paint on it. She wore bracelets thick as pipes, and
her hair was turning white, much whiter than
Castor's hair, as if she'd been shocked by what
she'd seen of the world.

'Some day,' she whispered to me later in the
kitchen 'you may want to see the desert.' I looked
into her grey eyes. She smelled nice and her voice
was soft and mesmerizing.

'In the Sahara,' she said, 'there are sand
storms, and sometimes it rains. It does rain.
Imagine,' she said, 'that you're sitting in a tea
house, at dusk, and suddenly along come men on
camels, dozens of them, beating them like this as
they ride past you … whoosh!' she swept her
hands past my face. 'Terrifying,' she grinned
widely. The woman had a strange power – I was
in love with Netty. We all were, all of a sudden,
in love with her. And today was the day we had
to go home.

Nothing can stroll quite like a horse. Its white
sides showed through the bushes and then it
stepped out onto the grass, strolling to the lake. It
dipped its muzzle in the water and I followed,
keeping a long leg's distance behind it, wondering
how it had got loose. It drank and shifted from
hoof to hoof, stepping deeper into the water until
it stood attached to its own reflection. I heard our
car start up, then stall, then there was quiet
again. The horse looked at me, a stream of water
running off its chin, and I got a feeling I get
sometimes. I wonder when we're all of us going
to disappear, go our separate ways, lose
everything. Netty disappearing. My mother

vanishing. As if the world would snap them away. I was feeling sorry for myself.

Behind me came a short laugh and footsteps. I turned to see my uncle come running, a wicked look on his face. The horse veered and dashed out of his way as he scooped me up into surprisingly strong arms and kept on running, over the grass, me screaming, him laughing. And then the two of us shot off the end of the dock and out over the water, our reflection moving like a space ship falling to earth.

Worse Than Taxi Driver

LIFE IS GOOD. I am sitting in a dim movie theatre with my father, drinking flat pop and eating licorice, and *Bambi* is about to come on. As soon as the movie starts, I know my father will fall asleep. The TV does the same thing to him; I think that is why he volunteers to take me to movies, so he can sleep.

I ask him now 'Fold or rise?' and he says 'Fold.' My father and I make bets on everything, and today it's whether the red phoney velvet curtain will be raised fold by fold, or will just wheel itself into the ceiling. But I should know better. My father has brought me here before and he remembers. I give my father the thumbs up for winning as the curtain flops and thumps its dusty way up and the short cartoons begin.

My exhausted mother is at home, lying across the double bed like she fell from a plane and my new little brother is asleep in the underwear drawer. They didn't buy a crib or changing table or anything until he was safely born because my mother is from a Scottish background and is extremely superstitious about things like that. In her family, no one will leave shoes on tables, or go out a different door than the one they came in, or say anything optimistic without trying to find a piece of wood to knock on. My father's awkwardness and general optimism sometimes leave her stunned, considering the disasters that she feels sure await them both.

And who knows, maybe she's right. Maybe the worst will happen if you wait long enough.

But today she is asleep, one hand extended to the underwear drawer which squirms and kicks with a new Andrew inside. My parents have been pouring as much attention on me as possible, ever since the neighbour lady gave me a doll. I thanked her nicely and went upstairs with it, where I was found later, shutting its head repeatedly in the bathroom door. My mother was very pregnant at the time and she and my father just looked at me. I pulled the doll's distorted head off and held it out to them.

So this is why we're at the movies, to keep me in a good mood so I don't kill the baby. The shorts are over and my father is already passed out, his hands on auto-pilot holding his drink and popcorn on his knees. I take a big slurp of pop and beam up at the screen. *Bambi!* Excellent!

But it's not very excellent. Pretty much right off the bat Bambi's mom gets shot dead by hunters. She murmurs a few survival tips to him, watches him play, and then whammo! she's gone. And as if that's not enough the whole forest bursts into flame and Bambi is nudging the corpse of his mother and staggering around in the inferno. It's the worst thing I've ever seen. I stare

in disbelief at the screen with my mouth hanging
open, my grip on the soft drink getting tighter
and tighter.

My father dreams about his brother, Bishop. In
this dream, Bishop stands on an ice field with the
aurora borealis flicking on and off overhead like a
bedroom light, and next to him is the
mountainous flank of a killed whale. Bishop's
mouth opens and a strange wailing comes out. It's
a horrible noise, torturing my father's ears, and
then it is joined by other voices, also wailing.

'Christ,' my father says out loud, 'why'd you
bother killing it then?' At that moment, my grip
caves in the cup of 7-Up and I geyser liquid over
both of us. My father wakes up and staggers down
the aisle with me, weeping and hysterical,
holding me out in front of him like a leaking bag
of groceries. He is followed by other parents with
a similar problem, their children perhaps
provoked by me.

To this day, I am unswayed in my conviction
that *Bambi* is worse than *Taxi Driver*.

* * *

'Isn't he a doll?' the woman shrieks. 'Isn't
he an absolute doll?' She's come over to bring
jams and baby clothes and she's just barely
concealing her shock at finding the baby in the
drawer. To cover up, she yells. Andrew has a
towel under his head and plastic pants on and
he's looking up at the bristle brush of shapes
leaning over him. I'm peering into the drawer
as well, poking a finger at his feet. They look
kind of comical to me, toes like corn niblets,
and so does the way the baby seems to goggle

at the world with his hair standing on end, as if he's never seen the like. The expression, we will discover later, comes from the fact that he badly needs glasses and can't see anything. He gawps at the shape of the lady now and gives it a grin. She goes off like a doorbell; there's more stuff about what an angel he is, and I have to leave the room.

II

I whine constantly these days. My mother says: if you must whine, go and do it on the porch. I'm caught in a logical bind; I can't seem to stop whining, but she won't let me do it around her, so I give up and go out onto the porch. This display so impresses my mother's friends that they go home and try it on their kids.

I want desperately to get out of the house. Right now I'm as fun as a rattlesnake. All my friends are away for the summer and I am alone on the street with nothing to look forward to but the arrival of my cousins. I have way too many cousins on my mother's side, none on my father's. This bunch comes in a station wagon and they all yell. The car door opens and the dog erupts from the car, then my cousins pour out like fish from a bucket.

It is clear to me that my life is either a misery or a bore and, for this, I blame Andrew. He's one and a half years old, and he's no fun at all. At the moment, he's only old enough to stagger around and pull things over onto himself; to scream at nothing and laugh at me when I jump; to throw things, with surprisingly good aim. Sometimes, I hand him a rock, then point him at other children, like a slingshot.

I sit and glare at my sandwich and grumble violence and death under my breath. My brother stares at me from his highchair. His hair is standing straight up and he holds a spoon which he has a fondness for clacking against his plastic tray. He points the spoon at me and says something very pointed and garbled.

'Holy mackinaw!' laughs my father, 'He spoke French!' He looks at Mum, 'We got a French baby by mistake.' My mother and I scowl, unimpressed, while the baby blows spit all over the table. The cousins arrive, then, thundering up the porch steps, one of my mother's many sisters laughing her head off. Andrew squeaks at the huge black shape approaching us all. I slip around the table and try to escape out the back door but am crushed beneath the feet of a Newfoundland dog.

It's been a night. They all agree, it's been a night, the dark lawn still flickering with the shapes of children. My father has found some sparklers and a boomerang and a long piece of nautical rope. My aunt says: 'Just don't hang anybody with it.'

They've moved the table out onto the porch and lit candles. My brother is half asleep under the table in a cardboard box; Mum has her bare feet inside the box, tapping her toe on his backside to keep him quiet. She looks out on the lawn, where someone tightrope walks along the fence and the girls spell their names against the dark with sparklers.

My mother thinks: life is good when you're
little. Then she remembers the sister next to her.
The two of them biting and punching and
whacking with brooms, burying alive, hanging off
banisters, jumping out of trees like Tarzan,
fighting silently and in a conspiracy of nastiness.
If an adult caught them, they would stand at
attention, furious, with throbbing lip and grass in
their hair. Fighting was private.

Her body remembers everything, too. After she
was married, a crazy old man had tried to kiss her
on the street and she had knocked him on his
seat before she knew what she had done.
'I'm so sorry,' she said helping him up, 'but
you shouldn't kiss strangers.'

She looks at her sister now, who is pink in the
cheeks with wine, and she can't decide whether
people change utterly over a lifetime, or don't
change at all. The two sisters are still competitive
in subtle ways: who drives faster, whose memory
is better, who saw a shooting star first. And the
past is never forgotten. Last Christmas my aunt
complained: 'It wasn't fair. You were always
Tarzan and I got stuck being the ape.'

III

I'm eight, lying in my room listening to
someone's nose buzz in their sleep. This is the
yearly visit again and we have all chosen to sleep
in my room, even Andrew, who sleeps in my bed.
His head points the other way and he's brought
his hockey pillow with him. We're badly
sunburnt, tired, and one of the cousins is allergic
to something, her nose buzzing and clicking.

Andrew sits up and his hand searches the bedside
table for his glasses.

'Hey,' he whispers, blinking at me through the
lenses.

'What?'

'Which would you rather eat, a dead squirrel or
a live snake?' Someone moans in his sleep.
Someone else, closer to the door, says, 'Dead
squirrel.'

'Okay, if you had to kill your best friend or
your parents, which would it be?'

Two voices now: 'Parents.'

'Oh, nice.'

'Okay,' Andrew goes on, 'what if you were ...'

The voices blither on and I slump down in the
bed, tune the sound out. You can get the feeling
that your parents are the only thing between you
and disaster. But that never lasts. People's parents
do die, there was a girl at school. I'm sure my
mother could fend off just about anything, but
sometimes I feel afraid for my dad – the way he
drives, like a bob-sled whipping along, his elbow
out the window. I had a dream that my father
froze to death, his car broken down in winter on a
lonely road. In the dream, no one would admit to
me that he ever existed. I woke up in a panic. He
was pulling apart both the dishwasher and the
lawnmower and I didn't want to let him out of
my sight. I told him jokes, asked him questions,
followed him back and forth between the two
mounds of wreckage.

I'm drifting off to sleep while Andrew and one
of the cousins discuss the merits of using high
voltage on the alligators who live in the sewers.
No one has noticed the nose-buzzer, who has

woken up and is currently crawling silently
across the floor towards my bed. In a moment,
just as the subject of giant spiders comes up, her
hand will seize my brother's leg though the
covers and Andrew will go off like a train whistle,
kicking me in the process.

Andrew's scream is legendary, he closes his
eyes and his little fists shake and when it's over
he grins, his cheeks crimson. Everyone wants to
hear it. The bigger kids, realizing that they only
get grunts and complaints if they hassle him,
have started paying; Andrew's been making some
good money at school. And in a moment, all of
us, the parents, the assorted dogs – perhaps even a
few neighbours – will be rigid and white-eyed,
hearing a small boy falling from the sky, falling
helpless through skyscrapers, dragging
catastrophe down on us all. And then silence,
followed by Andrew's low, kooky laugh, and the
weary thump of adult feet on the stairs. A house
full of pounding hearts.

Heaven Is a Place That Starts with H

ABOUT NINE O'CLOCK MY grandfather pulls up
in his convertible and says do I want to go to the
beach. I think that's great and I run to get in with
him – but then I see it. He's got a dead dog in the
back seat and when I say, 'What's that?' he says
it's Rufus, but he doesn't turn around. 'Aren't ya,
boy?' he asks, not looking at it. I'm just catching
the stink, when grandfather gets an idea: 'Race
you!' he shouts, stomps on the accelerator and
fish-tails down the street.

My mother looks up as I scramble past her
through the kitchen. She can hear the sound of
squealing tires outside.
'Was that Gerald?' she calls as I hit the back
porch, 'What's he doing?' But I don't answer; I'm
planning my perfect route to the beach road.

When I get there I can see grandfather in his
wide trunks standing in the water swishing it
into the air, all stiff-legged like it was the Arctic
Ocean. Then he makes a big whoop, and throws
himself in. The dog is still in the back seat and I
can picture him asking it if it wants to swim,
without ever looking at it.

My grandfather is paddling around in the
water. I go running in with my clothes on to
swim with him. It *is* cold as the Arctic Ocean. I
have this urge to run out again faster than I went
in, but I just float there, freezing. Grandfather
notices my face.

'What's the matter?'

'Caught my toe, that's all,' I say, gritting my
teeth. When we get out my lips are blue, a
sign my mother used to look for whenever we
went swimming. If that happens, you're about
to get hypothermia, she'd say. The thing my
mother finds so thrilling about hypothermia is
that you can still die even after they warm
you up. It's like your brain stays cold and then
dies slowly inside you while you sit there
drinking cocoa.

We get back in the car and grandfather
drives me back home, but I tell him I want to
go out for burgers instead and he thinks that's
great. He turns the engine off and we glide by
my house because my brother knows the
sound of the car and would come running out.
Then everybody would have to come and my
grandfather might be forced to do something
about the dog. It is getting kind of late and the
street lights are on, but the sun hasn't quite
disappeared yet. It kind of shoots out at you
between the houses.

'What do you want on your burger?'
grandfather asks.

'Onions, relish, tomato, mustard, ketchup,
lettuce, pickles, hot peppers, green peppers,
mayonnaise, salt and black pepper.' He turns to
the little speaker.

'Every damned thing you got.' The speaker

emits a crackle and a burst of gibberish and
grandfather says, 'Right.'

'I do calisthenics every day,' my grandfather
says between bites. We're in an open field and
grandfather has parked the car facing upwind.
'I sit on my bum. But I'm not fat.'
'You ought to exercise, even at your age. It
would build a good mind as well as a good body.'
'Everything I eat has sugar in it.'
'So?'
'So I might get overstimulated and have a
cardiac.'
'Really?'
'Really,' I say and wipe my chin.
'On top of that, Grandad, Andrew kicks me
every chance he gets and I can't stay in one place
that long. If I started doing sit-ups he'd be trying
to sit on my face.'
'Good point. You could always take up
running.'
'Flat feet.'
'No!' he says, looking pleased, 'You got that
from your grandmother. At least you have
something that makes you seem like family.'

I sit and think about that for a second.
'You mean I don't look like family?'
'Well,' he says and looks down on me, 'not
that you look ... well, you ... frankly no. I don't
know where you came from.'
'What! What do you mean?' He smiles and
bites away at his double-decker burger.
'Birth's a mystery,' he shrugs and I know he
isn't going to say anything more. I feel like
getting in the back with Rufus.

* * *

My brother is clamped to the TV, both arms
around it, his forehead pressed to the glass as he
stares at Rocketship Seven. Commander Tom
says 'Sit back, son, you'll ruin your eyes.'

'No,' my brother says in his little voice.
'Sit back, now. What if your mother walks in?'
'No,' he says and stares into Commander
Tom's soul.

It is seven in the morning, a beautiful day, not
a cloud in the sky and I come down to find my
grandmother sitting in our kitchen.

'I'm not going back until he gets rid of it,' she
says, embarrassing me with this honesty.
Children should never know about marital
problems. It just gives them ideas later on.

'I'm not going back.'

'You want some Eggos, Grandmama?' I ask.
My brother shouts, 'Me too!' from the other
room, and his breath clouds Rocky the Squirrel
for a second.

'What is he doing with it, the smelly thing?'
'Maybe he likes it.'

'Can't he like something if it's in the ground
instead of soaking into the Cadillac?' I know she's
not asking me. She's sort of pretending he's there
and she's talking to him.

I put a plate of waffles in front of my
grandmother.

'Blueberry,' I say, 'they're good.' She pokes at
the crusted edges with a long, slender finger,
scowls at the plate. The look on her face reminds
me of how I felt when I smelled the dog, Rufus,
standing in the sun beside the car.

'That dog sure smells,' I say.

'What dog?' Andrew calls, and my grandmother
covers her face and rushes from the room.

. . . .

'Andrew, let go the TV,' my mother says in
passing.

'No,' he says. She keeps going.

'What did your grandfather say to your
grandmother? She's all upset.'

'He didn't say anything.'

'When was he here?'

'He wasn't. Mum … can I have …' But she is
gone upstairs to tell my grandmother she's not
fooling anyone, she's making things up, who in
the world would keep a dead dog? I don't have a
chance to ask her for money. I ask for money
every morning and if I get it I go and buy as much
chocolate as I can. My brother takes his face away
from the TV to look at me and his hair sticks to it
with static.

'Andrew, let go the TV.' He thumps his
forehead back in place.

'No.'

* * *

I'm in the backyard trying to do sit-ups. I get
about three done before I feel my stomach start to
rip open. I stand up and hold onto it. Andrew
comes out back, his eyes like pinwheels.

'What're you doing?' he says, hoping I'd go
back to it so he could kick me or something.

'My gut just ripped.' I try not to move in case
all the intestines come tumbling out. I imagine it
looking like toothpaste when you spit it into the
sink.

'Did Grandad make you do that? Commander
Tom's a fascist. I ate Eggos for breakfast. Can you
sing with your mouth closed? A is for apple.'

'Andrew, go get Mum.'

'This is a test, do not adjust your Indian. Have
you seen the Breakaway Twins? Sound off at
eleven,' Andrew says as he goes back into the house.

'Hurry!' I yell and feel another little tear.

I know it then. Grandad's right. I am not really from this family. Something terrible happened at the hospital. It all starts to make sense, I mean, at school they always forget which one I am, and I've been there for four years! I could walk up in health class and get weighed and they'd say 'Well, Freddie, or whoever you are, you've lost weight *and* a couple of inches! Do you eat properly?' I bet I could do someone's tests for them and no one would know. What about babies that all look the same?

My mum comes down and sees me out on the grass.

'I was the wrong baby, wasn't I?' I yelled.

'What, in heaven's name, have you been doing?' she sighs and hustles me in to breakfast.

* * *

'Where'd the dog go, Grandad?' I ask. Andrew is standing with me beside the car as grandfather roars the engine.

'What dog?' says Andrew, looking up at me.

'God! That smelly thing!' grandfather bellows, 'I just looked around one day and couldn't believe it. He was *dead*!' He hit the steering wheel.

'What dog?' Andrew repeats.

'Is that boy all right?' grandfather asks, looking closely at him.

'I have twelve teeth. Heaven is a place that starts with H,' Andrew says.

'You know, young man, you're a little off-centre. You don't look much like your sister, either.'

'Grandfather ...' I want to stop him.

'Hospitals are terrible places, Andrew ...'

'Grandfather!'

'... and I think you got packaged wrong.'

'Prizes inside!' Andrew says, but he looks worried.

'Want to go for a burger, son?' he says, and off they go, Andrew holding onto the dashboard with both hands, pressing his face to the glass.

Bishop and the Aunties

THE ONE ABOUT THE birds is popular. Imagine
a cold summer in Halifax, a restlessness in all the
people, especially at night, and all summer an
arsonist is hard at work. Warehouses burn, shops
roll smoke into the windows of apartments
above, houseboats flame out along the shoreline,
drift away. Finally, the Port Haven bird sanctuary
down by the docks goes up. On that night, when
he's on leave from his troop ship, Bishop says, he
follows the smell of smoke to the huge glass
dome, and he finds it lit from inside by flame.
The shadows of birds, wild for escape, batter the
glass. The uppermost leaves of indoor trees wave
in the thick, convecting air; glass overheats,
bursts over the street; rag bodies of tropical birds
plummet through the night air, lie struggling on
the sidewalk, or pit the hoods of cars.

Andrew and I are paralysed as Bishop tells it,
his hands raised as if pointing out the horror. He
lowers his voice and tells us the air smelled good.
'Malarkey,' says my mother, 'he read that in
one of those awful boys' books.'

On a mild Tuesday in mid-summer, my uncle

. . . .

Bishop washed up on the river bank near his
home, barely alive. Perhaps it was a matter of
drinking as much as he did, and then not
remembering anything but shining stars, dogs as
big as houses that passed by growling at him,
voices coming from far off, maybe the voices of
the dead, and then fish. He was nudged head-first
into mud shore, burping and full of remorse,
strings of snotty weeds and twine and rotten
cloth draping his shoulders. It was a new story to
tell his grandkids, he reasoned, assuming he ever
got any; assuming he ever gets married.

That's the problem, anyway. He's had women,
one at a time, lined up over the years and each
one makes me and my brother call her 'auntie'.
My father's pretty much had it with Bishop and
his crazy women. With Bishop, he says, it just
goes on and on. My mother doesn't mind one way
or the other, and she says Dad should be thankful
he doesn't have any sisters.

All because of the most recent auntie, Bishop
got drunk, got beat up, and floated down the
river, so my father had to come and see he was all
right. She left him, took almost everything he
had, and said she didn't believe his stories
anymore. That's the worst slap in the face to
Bishop. His stories are his currency, his way in
the world. It had never occurred to me or my
brother that Bishop made things up. We didn't see
how he could invent things like that. Andrew's
always been a little scared of Bishop. Bishop the
dog-shooter, the barroom-clearer; Bishop the
noose expert. What my father says is, if it isn't all
true, it should be.

There's the one about him being in Brazil,

going into a bar and seeing that they decorated
the courtyard with some lost NASA equipment
that blew off course and landed in the mountains.
The bartender had taken the machine apart and
pulled out the long sheet of paper, with its
squiggles and signs of the weather and the stars.
He strung it from the ceiling like there was a
party going on. Bishop says he called NASA collect
and the next evening they came in black suits,
came through town like an invasion from Mars
and got everything back, every last screw. The
party was over. Bishop stood among the dripping
trees, regretting his phone call, looking up at the
stars and imagining a satellite burning to earth
with its precious bell of information, needles in
distress, recording every fiery moment.

You get to like him, my uncle, especially when
you're little and you need a story to go to sleep.
He's got a way of seeing the world, mostly as
something that surrounds and centres on him.
Bishop is in love with the possibilities of life. But
eventually it gets to his girlfriends.

In the evening, on the Monday the last one left
him, he walked to town, following the railway
tracks by the river. The pale river and the silver
line of the railway pass through the mountains
here together. Two lines tracing the dark valley,
one straight and man-made, the other wild,
uneven. And there, in the moonlight, was Bishop,
walking along the rail like a kid on a wall, going
to town, with firm plans to drink too much.

He doesn't remember exactly what happened,
but, in the early morning, someone threw my
uncle into the river after beating him up. My
father assures us; he can be annoying. It was

almost morning when he came to a stop, not
more than a mile from home, floating up like a
canoe, growling a church song through his
swollen lips and paddling with the feeble hands of
the near dead. Two boys ran down to the shore
and put Bishop in their wheelbarrow. They took
him home like a trophy, but their mother said he
had to go home, so they wheeled him back along
the trees to his house, one boy under each handle.
Bishop kicked at them and swore in all the
languages he'd learned, and they grew frightened
of his sputtering mouth and his muddy beard.
They dumped him like a delivery of cord wood
and ran away home, the wheelbarrow jumping in
the ruts.

* * *

In Bombay, as a young man, Bishop leaned from
the kitchen porthole of a luxury liner, rested his
tired arms on a load of soap, and listened to a
strange, constant hum coming from the city. It
intrigued him, this sound; not mechanical, not
the wind, no kind of sound he'd heard before. And
then his mind identified human voices, tens of
thousands of human voices, coming across the
water to him from markets and streets, spilling
out into the harbour. Andrew and I look at a globe
and, privately, we think of India as a noise. Those
voices followed him back to work and clamoured
in his head as he slept in the early afternoon sun.
Bishop, asleep in Bombay harbour. Bishop asleep
in the mud of the riverbank, hearing the voices of
children.

It's way past midnight and I am supposed to be
asleep, was asleep anyway, until I heard our car
pull up outside and I know my dad is home. He's
been visiting Bishop. My mother finds it vaguely

unnerving the way I can hear things, through
walls, doors, across great distances. Now, I half
doze and let the sounds of my father coming
upstairs form themselves into an image of him,
his coat over his shoulder, his shoulders bent. I
hear them in their room, talking about Bishop,
the aunties, a casserole, dogs, beer. Bishop is
becoming a story of his own.

It was dusk when Dad pulled up in his car,
steam coming from the grill and a not-again look
on his face, and Bishop waved his hand hello, all
jolly. He looked like the king of the mud clan,
with his fly undone. The two brothers sat in the
light of a lamp by the kitchen deeply breathing
the cold air that flows off the mountains and
picks up the scent of the river. They slouched
down in their chairs, cradled beers, and closed
their eyes, listening to an army of mosquitoes
hum outside the screens. Once in a while there
would be the sound of an animal, something big,
lapping at a puddle in the dark.

Bishop was talking about this woman, how
she winged a casserole at his head, and then
earlier, long ago, how she had looked and what
nice songs she sang when she thought no one
could hear. He said she'd been a nun once and she
sang in a grey habit with other nuns and played
the guitar badly. But she'd given all that up.

Still, she liked to get worked up on coffee and
church singing, which she attended undercover,
coming home like a tuning fork that won't stop
ringing, passing through the rooms of the house
one by one, as if looking for something. She had a
trick she did with her shoulder – she could grind
the joint so that it sounded like a galloping horse

– which used to make the sisters shiver. She grew one white hair, only one, an event which Bishop said he found creepy. She wasn't scared of any of the usual things, like snakes, or nuclear war, but she screamed if a light bulb blew out and left her in a dark room. She considered it a kind of ominous message.

This particular auntie claimed she had second sight, but it was a faculty she seemed to summon only to accuse him of cheating on her. She believed she could tell what colour hair the other girl had. In that regard, Bishop said, she was always wrong, but you never knew if that meant there was no girl, or that there was a girl, but she had got the hair colour wrong.

'Why don't clairvoyants ever use their power on the lotteries,' he asked her, 'why not do something useful?'

He also wanted to know why she no longer believed in his stories, and yet, being an ex-nun, she believed what he called 'the most outrageous yarn in history', about how one young woman managed to get herself pregnant. That's when she threw the casserole, and my father had to suggest Bishop got what he deserved. Bishop never cleans house, and it was still there on the wall; a silhouette of Bishop in tomato sauce.

'Now I'm alone,' Bishop said, 'single,' and he scratched at his mud-hardened cheek.

* * *

I am lying in my bed, in my room, but my mind is fabricating a strange, calm scene: my father and my uncle, in the shadows. Time has gone by without notice and tomorrow comes up silently like a bubble through water. Morning birds

appear and scrounge around in the bushes,
making the branches shake as if possessed. A
finger of light advances along the river, stirring,
stirring, digging up the clay shore.

'All these noisy birds,' my father says, his head
drooping. Bishop's voice is a hiss, carrying on as if
he'd never stopped talking, asking about my
mother, does she sing any songs? Does she ever
throw things? He wants to know how early kids
get up in the morning – what do you feed them?
He doesn't wait for answers, but worries on about
a life which is beyond him.

When the sun comes through the front door
and falls across their legs, the two brothers sit up
and hold their heads. Bishop staggers off into the
bathroom and quickly falls asleep in the tub,
where it is cool and the light is dim. My father
looks up to see two identical boys staring in at
him, filthy boys with green collars of dirt round
their throats. One of them swears at him in some
language, and in my father's mind it's Bishop
saying it. His head feels like a wet cardboard box.

'Piss off!' he barks and they both skitter off the
porch and stand in the road. Then one of them
starts to cry and they go home again. My father
pictures Bishop in a wheelbarrow, hanging over
the sides like an octopus. Bishop with his scars,
old and new, his fat lip, his choking snore from
the bathtub.

Something about Bishop, something nice
about him, is that he talks to dogs. Not just
'Come here' and 'Aren't you a good boy'. More
like 'Never trust a hammer, Toby, even if you
wedged the head last week'; more like 'It's a sad
world, Buster, your friends should have told you
so.' And the dogs stare at him and angle their

53

heads and whistle in their throats. Around where Bishop lives there are dogs that don't belong to anyone – perhaps eight of them – big dogs that all look the same. It's like they're a different species, my brother says, a race of giants that only come out at night to trot along the river banks and snap at fireflies and dig holes in the clay and rip each other's sides open. They come and go like raccoons at night and Bishop feeds them, sits alone in the light of a lamp and tosses old bread to the dark shapes moving beyond where the light falls. He talks to them, shouts at them, croons to them about what smart, sleek, beautiful dogs they are. At night they jam their noses against his screen door and puff at him, or sit by the river and yip and howl and the sound makes Bishop feel at home.

He's awake now, floating in the white of the bathtub.

'North,' he calls to my father, 'are you up yet?' He thinks the tub around him resembles the never-ending morning of the Arctic, blue sun reflecting everywhere – you can't escape it. He's listened to the ice sing and mutter, the hiss of dry snow moving in the wind. He's shot huge oily birds for food, shot caribou, shot dogs gone evil with hunger. His portrait is printed in *Life* magazine: Bishop standing by a Quonset hut blown inside out by wind, his face obscured by scarves and beard and fur. The caption reads: *This man saved my life.* Bishop squirms in his bathtub and remembers the last auntie shouting 'It's all such crap!'

'Hey,' he calls out to his brother, 'You there?' But my father is gone, having wiped strange paw prints from the hood of his car, slammed the door

and driven out to the highway. Mountains go up
both sides of the road and in the car my father
tries humming, which he always does when he
has a headache. The air is light and cool and the
tires flutter over the dry clay road. Dad slows
when he goes over a bridge and sees the syrupy
brown water where his brother passed like a
snapped branch, singing and moaning and calling
the last auntie by all her secret names. The
names he whispered in her ear, and in the ear of
the aunties before her, and in the ear of every
small child falling asleep dreaming of the Arctic
and the open sea and the many strange
possibilities of life.

Help Me, Jacques Cousteau

ALL THE LIGHTS IN THE house have gone out.
Andrew runs to the window, then turns and
heads out onto the street. He comes back in
saying everybody else has got lights in their
houses. I look over and see the upstairs lights are
still on. So's the TV. Jacques Cousteau is floating
in the living room, staring out at me and my
brother, and we are here in the dark, staring back
at him. A huge black shark floats by. Dad crashes
in the basement and swears long and
anatomically. There is silence and then another
crash. He's re-wiring the house again.

That was the day I stepped on a live wire,
came down the stairs ready to bother my dad, ask
him these riddles I'd memorized. I step down off
the last wooden step onto the concrete floor of
the basement and next thing I know I'm four feet
beyond, standing up, and all my fillings hurt.
'Jesus!' Dad says, shaking his head. 'That must
have hurt.' But I say no, and he relaxes, goes back
to work. I don't realize how addled I am, I tell
him my riddles, only I mix up the endings so they
make no sense. Dad laughs after each one
anyway.

He's digging in the fuse box, holding a mini flashlight in his teeth. He garbles something to me and points at the work bench. I figure it's the screwdriver he wants because it seems to be sitting in the only clear spot on the bench. I go to get it for him, step on the live wire again, leap, stand there watching the basement twinkle.

Jacques Cousteau is hiding behind a rock. Andrew runs to the TV and turns the volume up so high it hurts. We both like it that way. Jacques ducks as a dark shape glides by, and there are drums and tambourines and a screechy synthesizer somewhere in there with him. I grab Andrew's cereal away from him, and he fusses and whines, tries to grab it back until we hear Mum pull up in the car. It's like the starting shot in a horse race. Andrew tries to hide his cereal bowl under the couch, I jump up, snap the TV off, and run to the dark kitchen, look around at the wreckage I should have put in the sink long ago, Andrew skitters right by me and down the stairs to go hide in the laundry room. I hear him hit the bottom step, and then Dad's voice, 'Your sister did that, too.'

'That's it!' Mum is stamping across the floor. Between Andrew's panic about his cereal and me feeling guilty about the dishes I never do, I get ready for a real gale force, but she's not mad at me.

'I've had it with Annette Batter, absolutely had it!'

'Janey!' Dad calls from the basement. Mum's been visiting and she looks nice, a silky dress and ultra high heels.

'Janey, I'm down here.'

'If I hear one more thing out of her,' she starts, clicking carefully down the stairs in her fancy shoes, 'about that bloody fence, I'm going to strangle her; no, in fact North, I'm going to strangle you.' I run to the top of the stairs, watch her feet descend, getting closer to the bottom step.

'Mum, don't!' I call, 'Mum-Mum-Mum!' She steps down, the wire fitting perfectly into the finger's space under her high heel and she moves on unscathed. She turns.

'What, dear?'

I stare at her. How does she do these things?

'What is it, dear?'

'I forgot to do the dishes.'

'Do them now, then.' Then she turns to Dad and says could he please, please, please be more careful when he parks the car, if he cares for her sanity.

My father drives his Plymouth Valiant like a crazy man: jackrabbit starts, corners taken at such a speed that groceries roll like waves across the back seat. The brakes are given a good work-out, and he parks in one move, palming the steering wheel and craning his neck to look out the back window. The parking space we have is just exactly the size of our car and every night he shaves a slice off the neighbour's fence. Every morning, when the car leaps from the gravel and bolts out into the lane, he shaves off another slice.

The woman next door dislikes us because our dog got her dog pregnant about forty-seven times and, also, she's mad about the fence. The thing she finds so maddening is that Dad never does any damage to his own car. It's as if the Valiant is shaped perfectly to his task, the bumper poised, ready to peel her fence. Last year he tried to make up for it. He dug a new post hole and put in a new fence post, but she said it looked funny, stuck right out because it was new wood. He also sunk it right where the old one had been. The next morning, before he shot out into the lane way, he shaved a bit off that one too.

I run the water and start doing the dishes. It's quiet and I like the look of the soap bubbles in the dark. I splash around, flopping the soapy dishes up onto the drying rack. Both front and back doors are open and the dog comes clicking in the back door and heads for the front. Then he's gone again. Just as I'm finishing up I see a shape at the door, a small bulky shape in a striped shirt.

'Why's it so dark?'

It's Taylor. He's five. He's like someone put Popeye in a saucepan and boiled him down. He spits with perfect aim. He gooses me once in a while, seeing as he's down there anyway, and I have always suppressed my shocked reaction, thinking that he can't possibly know what he's doing. After all, he's only five. But it's wrong thinking.

'Where's the lights?' Taylor says again, and I tell him Dad's re-wiring the house. He hears Mum's laugh and his body gets all jumpy like an eager dog. Then he hears Andrew's voice and thumps across the floor, heads for the stairs.

'Taylor!' I shout, but then, soon enough, there's Dad's voice: 'Holy mackinaw! Did you see him jump?'

Big Blue Suit

AMONG THE FEW THINGS I know for sure about my mother, I've come to realize that she loathes weddings. Take the one this morning. The limo is out of control on the snowy road, spinning round and round. We're all screaming. The trees outside stutter past and the clouds go with them.

We're ten minutes from the church, and the weather has made us late already. The limo is crammed: there's me, my brother, Aunt Netty, my mother, Auntie Odelia, and Mrs Furstall, Odelia's mother, whom nobody likes. My mother has my fist in her hands and she holds it to her cheek in an iron grip. White balloons around our feet swirl and hip-hop up the window and hang there, suspended, until the car finally halts with a soft yank. The world is on a funny angle. My mother is rigid. Netty is trying not to fall over Odelia, who is by herself on the wide limo floor with her feet against the door. She is standing, effectively, on the door, hysterical, laughing and flapping her hands.

'Some driver you turned out to be,' Mrs

Furstall says to the limo driver, who must be about seventeen. He's trying to scrabble his way out of the front seat, pushing upwards at the long driver's-side door. Mrs Furstall, from her perch on top of the rest of us, swipes at his backside with her purse.

Odelia is another one of Bishop's women and, for some reason, she wants to marry him. That's why we're here, with our elbows in each other's ears. We all slide out the door, careful not to come out in a slithering bunch, dropping one by one into the snow in our pumps and stockings and silky dresses, all covered over with our crappy everyday overcoats. The bride-to-be is holding her wedding dress up high, to keep it out of the snow, and you can clearly see her elaborate black panties through the tight white hose. The sight reminds me of someone's face crammed against a window. She stares down in horror at the place where her legs disappear into the snow.
'Mother!' she wails.

This isn't the only wedding we've attended lately. There was the one in the fall – me in my horrible pink dress and Andrew in his oversized powder-blue suit. Heather, a friend of my mother's, was getting married for the second time, this time to a Scottish guy with an accent so thick, he must have stepped right off the hillside and onto a plane bound for Canada. The church was unheated, unadorned grey stone with a huge oak altar at the front and a life-sized, oak cross beyond. It put you in mind of a cold-storage room. We huddled in the front pews and my father blew his nose and the honk echoed around the walls. Then bagpipes bawled in the hallway, making our hair stand on end. We couldn't

understand a word of the service because the
minister mumbled; the groom was paralysed and
had to be coaxed; the bride giggled her vows and
pointed her toe behind her when kissed.

Finally, the bagpipes harried us all out of the
church and into the autumn leaves, where we
stood around under a lopsided tent, our noses
running and our lips blue. The groom's father sat
down with us and enthused incomprehensibly,
his voice rumbling, his rough hands spread out on
the table like two grey steaks. I had thought my
mother might enjoy herself, seeing as it was a
Scottish thing. On her side, my family are big
Highland people. But she hated it, especially the
kissing and the pointing toe.

'Heather used to be so forceful in school,' my
mother said. 'What in the world happens to
people?'

She says 'people' but she means 'women'. It's
not the emotion of a wedding that bothers my
mother, it's the ceremony itself, the sheer fact of
it, as if she's the only one who knows we're all on
the *Titanic*. She's superstitious; my mother is
secretly superstitious about everything. She
thinks of luck as a malevolent, watchful thing,
always present in your life. But it seems to be
more than just that. Not just bad luck –
something else, something worse. In this way she
is unlike any of her friends.

Gracey the librarian, for instance, is frustrated
that none of her girls are old enough to get
married. Angela and Gina are eight and twelve.
But Gracey plans ahead; she has a strong
inclination toward blue for the bridesmaids.

'Blue's unusual, I know,' she tells my mother

over the phone, 'but my Gina likes blue.'

'Gina's a baby,' says my mother, 'she doesn't even have her period.' Andrew, who has been listening, turns white and then red.

My mother is perplexed by people sometimes, disappointed by them. I try to figure her out, try to understand her in a real way. But at the heart of it, my mother is a mystery to me, and I believe, at the heart of it, she is a mystery to my father.

You can know basic things about my mother just by looking at her, like, that she's big; long and muscled and stately. Her feet are men's size ten, so she often can't find dress shoes in her size. She stands at parties in her stockings, a habit which gives people the false impression that she lives there. She is complimented on the furnishings, or asked for directions to the bathroom. My mother makes an airy gesture and says:

'Oh, over there.'

Her legs are long and slim and seem to come straight out of the ground, out of her feet and up until they get lost in her clothes. She has trouble finding shirts that fit her well.

'Pygmy clothes,' she mutters, scowling at blouses in stores, 'these wouldn't fit Andrew.' This attitude in her might account for the size of Andrew's formal clothes, as if one suit should suffice until he's old enough to buy his own. Growing is something my mother estimates poorly, having herself grown far too big, far too soon. She told me once that she grew fifteen inches in one semester; she would sometimes yelp in class, hold her arm or her thigh, which seemed to be tearing within itself.

Big Blue Suit

Without heels, she is as tall as my father, which makes her six two. She hates rainy days because umbrellas come at her eyes with their tiny metal spikes. She bumps her head and her shins when sleepy, stands on bent objects to straighten them. She bends over the counter in the kitchen – cutting tomatoes, tearing lettuce – leans back and cracks her neck, sighs. One of her wishes is for my father to build a higher counter top, but when can he do that, he says; *she* is always using the kitchen.

For kids, Dad will make things while they watch; Jacob's ladders, wooden swords and shields. There are kids all up and down the street who own boomerangs my father made from plywood, the angled surfaces carefully sanded and shaped.

Another thing I know about my mother is that she's quite strong. I hand her the jar of spaghetti sauce to open, and she pops it and hands it back. Baking a cake, she holds the bowl of batter in the crook of her arm and whips with a spoon, her arm flexed, never stopping or slowing or changing direction. Dad gets her to brace things while he hammers, hold ladders on which he teeters and reels, catch the ends of pine planks as they drop away from the screaming saw blade. She clamps her eyes shut and then, when her part is over, walks away rattling a finger in her ear.

My mother is practical, whereas I am not. Neither is my dad. He'll take two machines apart to fix them, then mix up the pieces. I'm worse than him; I can forget my wallet at home, go back to get it, and on the way leave my school books on the bus. Mum, on the other hand, can reach

into her bag and bring out anything she needs:
tape, a screwdriver, a spoon, note paper, scissors,
coffee, sugar packets, an eraser, elastic bands. She
uses the screwdriver to jimmy the back door
because Dad always locks her out. She uses the
note paper to abuse him about it, taping snarky
messages to his windshield.

She has a voice which is so like the one inside
my own head, I can never remember its exact
sound. She and Dad take turns reading books to
Andrew at bedtime, as they did to me when I was
young. At night, I listen to her spreading the story
out, soothing Andrew to sleep, her own existence
disappearing into the many forests and river beds
and snow-covered plains, the hovels and caves,
the bad sisters, the evil witches and all the tall,
beautiful men. She sits upright on a chair beside
Andrew's bed, leaning toward the light,
unimpressed by what she reads, privately
extracting from each story the dynamics between
men and women, the perverse lessons being
delivered, the critical warnings that are withheld.

She tells my father that the Little Mermaid is
an evil pile of nonsense, and the Ugly Duckling is
for saps. It's mean, she says, to suggest to ugly
little kids that some day they'll walk into a room
and all heads will turn and they'll instantly get
dates and end up on TV. My mother says we all
have to face facts, eventually.

My mother is the only one who slams doors in
our house. It's not an angry gesture, though, it's
just her excess energy. She whangs the car door
shut, deafening the rest of us. She elbows the
fridge door shut and jars within rattle in muffled
complaint. She walks out the front door and pulls

it shut behind her and the frame lets go a few
more slivers. The slivers fall down through the
air and land on little piles of other slivers; this is
how archaeology happens, layer after layer of
what happened, falling down and, after a time,
covering each other up. Facts, hidden away.

Like the fact that she left when I was very
little. No one told me, but I know something
about that, having heard half-finished references
to it through walls and doors, the silent challenge
of man to woman, or woman to man, the strange
unequal dialogue between unequal people. I know
that she was gone for a week. I know that she
took the white car. I know she came back,
missing her husband, lost without her baby, came
back in a different car, not the white one
anymore, but our green Valiant.

I look in the photo album, at the one picture of
a white car, just the back end of it in the frame, a
dog looking at the camera, and my grandfather
laughing, and my mother's long tanned arm
reaching in from nowhere, reaching for the dog. I
look at that photo the same way people look at
the lines on their palms, trying to analyse the
signature hidden there.

Bad luck hiding in your life, masquerading as
something simple, something pleasant – my
mother seems assailed by these shadows.

This winter there's been a ton of bad-luck
winter weddings, the cold seeping into churches
through coloured glass and loose doors, people
hustling through the vows. My mother has been
in agony, and Andrew and I haven't been too
happy either, what with the dreadful clothes,

worn and dry cleaned and worn again. My mother
made my father promise: no more commitments.
But then, there was the girl down the street who
was visibly pregnant. We had to go to that one or
people might think we were stuck up. At the
reception, the bride's father and the groom's
brother got into a slug-fest that rocked two tables,
crossed the dance floor and spilled out into the
hotel lobby, where it was stopped dead by a large
doorman in a top hat. After that one, my mother
said she had trouble relaxing. She took all the
iron heating grates out of the walls and scrubbed
them until the paint was thin.

My mother tries to be rational and logical,
tries not to let us see the many times she leans
over and surreptitiously touches wood.

'Superstition is a terrible thing,' she says, 'and
I'm glad I haven't infected you kids with it.' But
Andrew thinks stepping on a crack will break his
mother's back – so do all little kids. He also
believes that a hat on a bed will get someone
killed.

'Where did he get that?' I ask her.

'Not from me,' she says, sounding unsure. As
for me, I believe all bad luck comes in threes,
except for the kind that comes in fours.

One night Andrew dreamed that grandfather
died at sea, drowned in the thick, black waves,
and he woke up shouting for someone to help.

'Don't worry,' my father said, holding and
rocking him, 'your grandfather would never die,
he's too much of a bast....'

'North!' my mother says.

'Well, it's true! He's stubborn, and anyway, he
floats. All old men do.' The next day, Mum
worries about grandfather, as if my dad's flippant

. . . .

talk will bring on some kind of disaster.

'*Think* how we'd feel if something did happen to him,' she says.

'Sure,' my father says, 'I'd feel terrible.'

But the next day is my fifteenth birthday and we're out in the back yard with paper hats on. There are streamers strung along the fence, snarling together in the breeze. There is a howl of tires as my grandfather arrives to celebrate. He has a long scrape down one side of his Cadillac. There is also a bag full of my granny's dresses in the back seat which he pushes me into trying on one after the other. His birthday gift to me.

'There,' he bellows, as I stand before him in polyester paisley, 'doesn't she look fine in that?' I gaze down at the unravelling hem whiffling in the breeze. I look up again and see my mother, her eyes locked on my father. She's decided he's to blame for it, but she hasn't figured out how, exactly. Andrew comes crashing out of the house, skips down the steps and hugs grandfather's leg.

My father is aware of his place in this system of trouble. There's his family – that alone would do it. Then there's his ability to sleep through anything; movies, bad parties, weddings. Then there are all the little mistakes he has made; like the time he washed his gardening shoes in the kitchen sink, the smell of dinner combining with the odour of warm fertilizer. He looked up, the shoe suspended over the drain and noticed my mother's horrified expression.

'What?' he said, furiously trying to bluff her out, 'Do you want me to track this stuff through the house?'

Sometimes I agree with him, or perhaps I just decided to agree with his side of the unspoken, fuming dialogue of body language. They refuse to fight in front of Andrew and me. They think that makes things better. But in the end, it's just the same. Sometimes I feel sorry for my mother.

'I could call Connie,' she says, looking at the phone, or: 'It's been ages since I called mother.'

But in Mum's family you don't spend money on phone calls; you save it up and come for a visit. That's why we never see them. To my mother's mother, long distance means one thing: someone died. On the other hand, you never know when my father's family might come walking up the drive, no gift, no warning, no particular plans to leave. There have been times when we came home to find someone in the bath, or my grandfather rifling through my parents' drawers.

She says that when she was little, growing up on the prairies, she would walk out into the field and not stop until she knew she was too small to be seen.

'The thing I liked most in the world,' she tells me, 'was to just be quiet somewhere, in a field or under some trees, and no one in the world knew where I was.'

I think about my mother, stuck here with all of us, all our stories and fibs and downright lies, our troubled course through life, and today, Uncle Bishop getting married for no reason. Bishop and his new woman, Auntie Odelia, hysterical and up to her shins in snow; a limo in a ditch; my poor mother looking around her in shock.

Big Blue Suit

We hurry along the winding road in the snow,
an assortment of bonbons in frilly wrappings,
Andrew tugging at his light blue suit, lost in it
like a boy in a bag. My father and I cornered him
after breakfast and wrestled him into his pants.
Once they were on him, he was like a broken
horse, allowing us to slip the jacket on, do up the
top collar button, tighten the little tie. He stood
there in the hall, trussed up and glaring, a living
indictment to us all.

Inside the church, we look for a place to hang
our coats and, right away, I see what seems like a
little closet against the wall.

'There, look!' I say and am well on my way
before my father snaps me back by the upper arm.

'That's a *confessional*,' he hisses.

That was how the wedding began, and it went
on in a kind of fluttering rush from badly played
organ music, to the wobbly-kneed bride, fainting
finally and finishing her vows from the floor. The
bridal corsage exploded in the icy wind, leaving
nothing but stems, tossed backwards over the
bride's shoulder, and directly into the eye of Mrs
Furstall, on whom, my grandfather said, the
promise of being the next to be married was
clearly wasted. On we went in a giddy race until
it was mercifully over, people driving into the
darkness loosening ties, kicking off shoes.

My mother sat upright behind the wheel, her
eyes wide and white in the rear-view. My father
slept, just as he had slept through the service, the
alcoholic reception, the shrill dispute between
grandfather and Odelia, the bride's storming out,
and Mrs Furstall's final, acid summation of our
family character. We drove and traced the

headlights wearily through the dark, and when
we pulled up behind the house, my mother sat
slumped with her head back on the wide bench
seat and the overhead light beaming weakly on
her face. We left her to whatever thoughts she
might have, uneasy in our own hearts and
wanting to get away. Dad carried Andrew into the
house, fast asleep and slithery in his loose suit
like a fish in plastic, only to find Bishop, alone,
passed out in his tux on our couch.

I saw my father's expression before I saw
Bishop. I imagine that in the split-second before a
car-wreck people have that look on their faces. At
that moment, I saw the future clearly, recognized
the shape of it, the wild and treacherous promise,
the way it lay out before us now and had always
been nearby, and I saw that many of the things I
feared were there.

Bigfoot

MY GRANDFATHER IS STANDING in his housecoat, which he calls his smoking jacket. It's got guns and dogs and panicking pheasants all over it. On the table in front of him are burnt hamburgers, burnt buns; somehow I even let the pickles dry into little green tongues. My grandmother tells him I made dinner – sit down and eat, what's the problem – but he doesn't move.

'Well, yes ...' Grandfather starts.
'Sit down,' Grandmother says again.
'Do you know that I've eaten mastodon?' my grandfather says, shifting from foot to foot. We've all heard this story before, and we ignore him, fiddle with our burgers, discover that the buns are really quite edible on their own. Grandfather sits down.
'Do you know what a mastodon is, Andrew?' he asks and Andrew stares at him with open fatigue.
'He's making this up,' my grandmother says, 'there never was any mastodon.'

She is sitting back, her hands in her lap,

staring at her plate. Her hair is white-blond, like corn silk, and swept back off her forehead. Her eyes are very blue.

My brother and I have heard this story before, and we've heard our grandmother's versions, which are numerous and have nothing in common except that they are the negatives of his. That's what their relationship is like; whatever he says, she says it isn't true, even on the occasions that it might be true.

Since my parents left, I sleep in Andrew's room laid out on the floor on an air mattress. Andrew claims that I shout and laugh in my sleep and, from the looks of him in the mornings, maybe I do. My grandfather is sleeping in my room and my grandmother is in our parents' room. They creak back and forth during the night, visiting each other, whispering. I sit up late, reading poetry and scrawling in my notebooks, and I can see my grandfather's shadow move across the crack under my door. The floorboards bend under his weight. I can't see him, but I know he's wearing Dad's blue dressing gown, with teeth marks at the hem from the dog. At night, Grandfather paces and knocks around in my room, then creaks down the hall to see my grandmother. They don't know it, but I can hear what they're saying; they are discussing my parents. After a while, I plug my ears.

According to family history, my grandparents spent their honeymoon in Russia during the first five-year plan. Granny says that at midday on the day they arrived, the Moscow sun was weak and bluish, and the air was dull-smelling, like hot metal. She pronounced the food delicious and

gained twelve pounds, but Grandfather poked at
things, left his plate full. In one restaurant, he
complained about the listed price for fish and, to
his shock, everyone shouted at him at once,
including the cook. He claims that Russians
applaud in unison. At intermission, play-goers
walk in circles, in a clockwise direction. There is
no discernible division between a sidewalk and
the street. The Russians, he decided, are big on
togetherness.

Nineteen-thirty-something. That's when the
mastodon was found, emerging whole from a
glacial wall, preserved and impossibly huge. And
before the scientists could get there, relics were
taken, steaks cut, hide removed, the waist-thick
tusk sawn off as close to the ice as possible. I
imagine the mastodon entering the air shoulder
first from a glacier, eyes cloudy, and people
standing around, examining the dubious shape,
the drip and stream of melting matter. I imagine
the smell.

But it's all crap, really. These days, I don't
believe him any more than she does.

And that's what bothers me: why don't I? It's
not like I'm above believing stuff like that. My
uncle Bishop is far worse, wading around in his
own subconscious world of tall tales. Even my
father, on the odd occasion, throws fact to the
wind and just makes things up.

I have to stay away from grocery store tabloids
because the crazy ideas stick with me. I
remember them in detail: Elvis, JFK, Jackie
Onassis. Walking trees, blood baths, Satan,
impossible babies. It's hard to fight the desire for

it all to be true. I sit watching movies made especially for fools like me, my mouth hanging open: *The Exorcist, Rosemary's Baby*. They enter my dreams, woven together in surreal combination, and I wake with a desire to check myself for marks and signs. Good Kirk fighting bad Kirk in the vestibule of time. Body Snatchers growing in the pumpkin patch. HAL the computer can lip-read.

And yet, my grandfather can tell me he swam in the lake last night, and I won't believe him.

I keep Andrew up at night, shining the light in his face to keep him talking. My brother accepts the family history according to Grandfather, the picture of us all that he creates, all the things he insists are true and solid and real. To Andrew, questioning that is like wondering if the dog bites. Sure he does.

My dad calls from somewhere up north and his voice is thin and strung out. My mother is in a coffee shop across the highway, he says, so we just speak to him. I can hear trucks going by in the background. My parents have gone for a long drive to talk things out. When my grandmother takes the phone I hear his voice like a mosquito, but I can understand every word. Dad calls his mother 'mother' and his father 'father'. He thanks them for looking after Andrew and me and asks if we're behaving. When it is over, Andrew goes up to his room and closes the door and stares unseeing at a comic. I go outside.

For the next few nights I dream about trucks, about driving into the dark with the huge truck going crazy under me, skidding around and missing trees. Andrew and I both wake up the same way every morning: it takes a moment or two, but then we realize we're still stuck with our lives.

To keep busy, my grandmother is trying to teach me a few useful things, like cooking and using a sewing machine. Last summer it was knitting, which is one of the few things she doesn't do very well. I took to it like it was something illicit and knitted everybody something absurd for Christmas. My mother got a tank top made of butcher's string. My best friend, Jeannie, got a pair of wool boxers with tinsel and chestnuts worked into the pattern. Jeannie put it up on her wall and her mother told her I was crazy.

This anarchy wasn't what my grandmother had in mind. So, she is trying now with sewing. But I snarl the thread into pom-poms and run the needle through the edge of my finger. Predictably, my performance in the kitchen is no better.

My grandfather reads the paper and complains that Andrew isn't small enough to sit on his knee anymore. He acts like Andrew did it on purpose. Once in a while, he goads my brother into trying again and then makes a big deal about how his leg almost broke. Before they arrived, I collected all my poems and notebooks and old childhood drawings of other planets and I hid them behind the furnace. I thought I was safe then. But, the first morning, Grandfather came down holding one of my earrings – a silver fish-skeleton. He wondered out loud whether he couldn't find a dead cat for me to wear around my neck. The earring is gone, perhaps dropped by him in a garbage bag, ten bucks down the drain. It bugs me

. . . .

sometimes, when I consider the appalling things he wears.

Andrew is outside with a bunch of other little boys. They are popping the top off a yogurt cup by combining baking soda and vinegar. This is explosion number five. The littlest boy is standing with one sandal on the lid and they are all shrieking with excitement. I can hear my grandmother in the kitchen, going through the cupboards, irritated about something. It is a warm, airless day. Cloud has settled low in the sky. There are puddles forming in the narrow alleyways between houses, spiders string their webs everywhere, and the branches of the highest trees look rotten and wet.

My grandmother is planning to teach me to bake a cake this afternoon, lemon cake, my favourite. But today I can't stand it. I just want to be alone. A series of images flies through my mind. A roast chicken, white as my underarm, hard as a rock, with stuffing extruding out its rear end like wet sand; a Jell-O mould with sockets where the cherries slid out; a cream of mushroom soup that smelled like a rainy ashtray. I'm not sure I can stand another moment of it, my grandmother's smooth graceful hands taking the bowl away from me, whipping the batter with stunning speed and, despite her efforts, the cake coming out stunted and gooey, with my name written all over it.

And then it hits me: no cake today. Andrew has exploded all the baking soda. I see the yogurt cup spurting and hissing like a sick toad on the sidewalk and little boys screaming, kicking it. My grandmother comes thumping across the

carpet to see what the noise is and so I hit the
road out the back door. All I want is to lie in the
back seat of their Cadillac and read poems or
watch the clouds sink lower and lower.

Like so many of the other things he sorts and
compares and commits to memory, my father has
a fondness for weather. He collects magazine
pictures of tidal waves and tornadoes and sheet
lightning. He has photos of storm fronts on the
prairies, moving toward the camera like grey
walls. He has photos of clouds forming over
mountains, slide after slide of cirrus, nimbus,
cumulus. Clouds that resemble the sand in
shallow water or the waves in a girl's hair. Clouds
that bulge like muscle, or streak and ribbon.

In his classroom at Willow Heights High
School, there are aerial shots of Mount St. Helen's
exploding, diagrams of the directional forces
inside twisters, a map showing the incidence of
human deaths caused by lightning. Rangers get
hit a lot. They hold up blasted hats as proof for
photographers, complain of bald spots, ringing
cars, a leg that won't stop trembling. Women
almost never get hit because, unlike men, they
opt not to adjust the TV aerial in a storm. Dad
says, you can feel lightning coming, a tingle in
your feet and calves, a searing in your mouth. If
this happens, he says, throw yourself down and
roll on the ground. Lightning comes from two
directions, the ground and the sky.
    'Like any current,' he says, 'two sides must
connect or nothing happens.'

I remember him running his fingertip along a
flickering fluorescent tube at school, the blue
flashes following his finger to the other end and

the tube snapping on. I remember him counting between the lightning and the thunder, saying every fourteen beats is one mile. Or maybe it was every beat is fourteen miles? I can't remember.

I lie in the car and look up and hear a thin rumble come across the sky, without a flicker of light from anywhere. I put the convertible top up and listen for the sound of rain on the tattered black canvas.

I'm feeling bad about Andrew. I should be helping him somehow, but I can't even help myself. Last night, he wanted to know if I thought Dad and Mum were going to split up, and I told him to shut up. It popped out so fast and mean that I surprised myself, I couldn't even say sorry. He was quiet for a long time, holding on to his covers. And then he said, 'Where's the coffee shop?'
  'What?'
  'Where Mum was.'
  'Who knows, Andrew? Who cares?'

It's funny how your mind works. Someone says don't think about dogs and suddenly your mind is filled with dogs. I knew where my mother was. I could see it. The walls were white, the tables brown, she was smoking and there was a man coming along the row of tables with a pot of oily coffee. There were trucks parked outside and people leaning on cars, filling their tanks at the pumps. My mother was watching my father's shape in the phone booth, and he was looking back at her shape in the window of the café.

How stupid could I be? I get fooled by things all the time. I believe Bigfoot exists, I really do.

. . . .

But these things are easy to imagine, because
they don't have to be true; it isn't important. I
feel bad about my brother, because, for him, some
impossible things have to be true.

It's getting dark out, and the lights from the
house illuminate the inside of the convertible
roof. Rain pelts down on the car and things feel
different, like I might have fallen asleep without
noticing. Gradually, it comes to me that I've been
asleep with my book lying open on my stomach.
There is a radio playing somewhere nearby and so
I sit up to see what is going on.

'Oh, Jesus God!' My grandfather screws
himself round in the front seat. 'Where did you
come from?' The baseball game is on and he's
sitting there in his white undershirt and bathing
trunks. He's soaked with rain and he looks happy,
or he would look happy if he wasn't holding his
chest against a heart attack.

'I've been asleep, Grandfather,' I croak, quickly
sitting on the poetry book.

'What have you got there?' he snaps right
away. Reluctantly, I hand e.e. cummings over to
him. He opens it and stares, then reads out loud.

'"i sing of Olaf glad and big / whose warmest
heart recoiled at war: / a conscientious object-or"
... What is that? I don't think that's poetry.
Object-or?'

'Grandfather ...' I try to take the book back,
but he holds it out of my reach.

'... "to eat flowers and not to be afraid?" Uh-
boy.'

He hugs the book close to himself and keeps
reading. Rain pelts the car and I watch it drool off
the tops of the windows and confuse the image of

our back fence. I'm getting used to this. Kids at
school make fun of everything everybody does.
Reading poetry isn't so bad; at least I don't have
huge boobs, or flood pants, or a case of acne. I'm
not in the chess club. I don't have a name like
Bogdana or Flower. Things could be worse.

'That one's not bad,' he says, poking a page,
and then he gives the book back to me and sits
still for a moment, holding the wheel. He taps at
the glass over the red brake indicator.
   'Do you know that I used to write poetry?'
   'Before or after you ate mastodon?'
   'Never mind, then.' He shuffles around and
snaps his waistband, annoyed.
   'Granny told me.'
   'Huh, … well,' he says. Actually she'd showed
me some of Grandfather's poetry, and it wasn't
embarrassing, in fact some of it didn't rhyme.
From the looks of it, he'd written a ton. They
were all dedicated to her, and not one was about
love. He shifts in his seat a little, then turns the
radio up louder and we listen to the Blue Jays and
the Angels get rained out.

When we come in for dinner Andrew is in the
kitchen alone. He is standing on a chair stirring a
pot of soup. The kitchen is dark. Grandfather and
I stand in the hall and look at the shape of my
brother cooking, a diminishing glow coming from
under the soup pot.
   'We blew a fuse,' Andrew says without looking
up. Then the lights come back on and we can see
that Andrew has the apron doubled up and tied
high under his arm pits, so he won't trip on it. My
grandmother can be heard, making her way up
the basement stairs and Grandfather hotfoots it
up to my bedroom to change out of his bathing

trunks before she catches sight of him. She
wouldn't have said anything to him of course. She
wouldn't have to.

I look at my grandmother where she stands at
the head of the stairs with her hands on her hips.

'Your father did a decent job on that wiring.'
Andrew and I gawk at her. Those were the most
unlikely words to be spoken in our house, under
the circumstances. My father re-wires things
when he's nervous, and he's been very nervous
lately. It occurred to me that my grandmother,
between teaching my father how to cook and sew,
might have given him practical home
improvement lessons as well.

The food smells great and we all sit down
together to a delicious meal cooked by Andrew.
He's at the head of the table, spooning the soup
into bowls, hacking at the chicken and passing
out beautiful, white, uneven slices. He stirs the
gravy, and spoons out beans and potatoes. It's the
nicest meal we've had in a long time, and I go to
bed with a new respect for my brother.

As usual, my dreams buck and roll under me.
When you sleep, you are sometimes aware of
everything; the fact that you are dreaming, the
room around you, the strange logic of your own
dreams. I can hear Andrew breathing the way
little boys do when they are exhausted. I can
sense my grandfather moving in the hallway, and
yet I am horrified at the ground under my feet,
swelling and breathing like a living thing. I know
that, soon, I will fall off and see whatever this
thing is, as clearly as an insect sees a shoe. But
when it happens, as the bed sinks away to
nothing, I find that I am awake. Birds are coming

out in the trees and a weak yellow sun filters
through the window. I sit up and stare at my
brother, who is small and pretty and restful.

For a long time I've had the strange idea that
we were born the wrong way around. He should
have been born first, born female and given to my
grandmother, who always wanted a daughter, but
got boys instead. My brother should have been
me. And I should have been born later, and male.

Of course, years later, when my brother grew
huge and muscular and bearded, and left home in
a truck to go to college, that idea would seem
absurd. But right now it strikes me as horribly
true. My parents are gone, shot into orbit by
something out of our control, and my
grandparents roam through our lives in their own
perplexing patterns. How would it be, that other
life? I lie back and watch the sun come across the
ceiling and I picture things as they might be,
picture myself as a boy, and it's not exactly hard. I
don't tell myself that things might be better. I
don't tell myself anything at all.

Fish-Sitting

MY BROTHER HAS STOPPED TALKING. All he
does now is read; kids' books, adult books,
newspapers, the cereal box, pill bottles, signs,
advertisements and scrawls on the sidewalk. He's
the best reader in his class, but they can't make
him talk. I'm looking at him now, lying on his
stomach on the living room rug.

'What're you reading, Andrew?' I say. But he
just holds it up: *Asterix*.

I go back to spying on the new neighbours
with the binoculars. The new neighbour lady,
Mrs Draper, is out, drinking on the grass of her
back yard with someone who isn't her husband.
In this way, she is just like the previous
neighbour lady. My mother says that maybe it's
something about the house itself, like a gas that
comes out of the basement and makes people
crazy. She's convinced Mrs Draper is having an
affair with this man, and it looks like she's right.
Mrs Draper has her foot up on his thigh and she
lets her head fall back, sun beaming on her neck.
He's rubbing her ankle and touching her leg. He's
got his back turned to me, but I can see the
orange hair under his baseball cap, and on his

forearm. He leans over and retrieves the bottle from under her chair. With Mr Draper the way he is, I'm not surprised she's opted for this.

I can also see my father out there, talking to the Bison. I call him the Bison because he's got this huge head with woolly hair that starts too far back. I imagine a sci-fi world where everybody looks like that. He's kind of shuffling around on his front mat, the blare of sunset throwing his lumpy shadow across the front door. My dad's at it again, I can tell by his expression; open, fatherly. The Bison is spilling his guts.

When Dad comes in I say 'What did he tell you?' Andrew glances up at Dad, wiggles his nose to adjust his glasses.

'The Bison? Oh, well, he's worried about selling junk bonds, mostly because it's just a disgusting thing to do, he's attracted to Mrs Shiffler down at the corner, and ... um, I think that's all. Oh, ya, his first sexual encounter was with his cousin.'

That's my father, these days. He's spending more time talking to people, mostly because he can't talk to Mum, and as time goes by, he's getting better at it. People seem to trust him, to want to confide in him; he's the stranger on a train. They take one look at him and decide it would be much better to get that niggling little secret out in the open. Men confess to impotence, cheating on their taxes, a desire to drive into on-coming traffic. One lady confessed to poisoning her husband's dog because he always kissed it on the lips. 'It was,' she said, 'repulsive.'

It was good to find out how really warped

other people were, because our own home life
was a mess. My parents had decided to separate
and my mother was moving out. We were all kind
of floating because, even though the change had
come, nothing yet had happened. This was a time
when I wasn't doing too well in school. I don't
know what it was, but I felt like summer had
come all of a sudden and I had nowhere to go and
nothing important to do. My dad would take me
aside and do his best to scare the shit out of me
about what happens when you let yourself go, but
I still felt like it was something other people had
to care about. I'd sit in class and enjoy the sound
of talking, but I wasn't really there. Some of my
teachers worried about me. I saw their mouths
move, but it didn't occur to me to wonder what
they were saying. And then at night I'd stay up
late and stare through the binoculars.

Sometimes, walking along the street, I'd pass by
a face I'd been spying on and it was hard not to say
hello. Or worse, to say something like: 'How's the
zit cream coming?' or 'Why do you let that cat lick
your toes?' It's true, there was a woman who put
her feet out on the coffee table and her cat got up
and licked her toes. I'd go through the roof.

* * *

It's ten o'clock at night, and I see Mr Draper
coming up the drive to his house. He swaggers,
fumbles with the key. In the dark he lets a bottle
drop on the stoop. She's locked him out again. I
can see his shape from where I sit in my room
with the lights off, and I watch as he disappears
into the house leaving the door ajar. In a minute
she comes out with a dustpan and pokes the
shards of glass onto it with a fingernail. Then
she's gone and the door is still open, the light

from inside glistening in the pool of booze. I can tell something's going on downstairs. It's pretty quiet as usual, no raised voices. My brother comes in and sits on my bed with a book; sometimes he crawls under the bed and reads with only his head and shoulders sticking out.

My mid-term report is a wall of rejection, and what's worse is my dad can see that I don't care. My parents are like wolves working as a team to pull something down. This is one of the rare moments when they co-operate in anything and I sit there mostly admiring their self-control. I know I'm a pain in the ass. I know I should be promising things, acknowledging faults or at least trying to look worried. But I can't even manage that.

We're in the kitchen, with the back door open and a lawnmower droning away somewhere. I sit there on auto-pilot as usual, watching their mouths move, listening to the grinding machine like it might tell me something useful. When I come back into focus my father is sitting back, looking satisfied. My mother gives me a kiss on the forehead and then leaves the room. I realize that I've agreed to something, but I have no idea what it is. Two days later, Mum gives me a book from the library on tropical fish. 'I thought this might help,' she says. I tell her thanks. Apparently, I've agreed to do something about fish.

I've always hated school, but now even my girlfriends there are acting like I've got some illness they don't want to catch. We're sitting at a greasy spoon eating fries and gravy, drinking coffee.

Fish-Sitting

'You know,' Ginger says, 'you used to be a lot more fun.' I can tell she's angry for some reason, glaring at me, stabbing her fries in Rosalie's gravy. It's obvious they've been talking about this, because Rosalie looks panicked, like she's thinking maybe she'll go to the washroom right about now.

'You spend too much time with Marty. I don't know what you think is so great about Marty. She's not a normal person.'

'What do you want me to say?' I ask and it's a real question. But Ginger doesn't take it that way.

'See? That's what I mean. You think it's everybody else's problem. You totally change, and it's everybody else that's screwed up, right?'

Rosalie jumps in to save me and tells Ginger to lighten up, what's the point in getting upset, and those are the last words I hear, because I tune out again. I know that if Rosalie wasn't here, Ginger would be pulling out the big guns and talking about my parents, maybe saying I'm unbalanced because of it, or maybe that it's my fault what's happening to them, and to me. Everything she says is familiar, and it all translates into: you are getting on people's nerves. I watch the cook scrape the grill with a spatula, the oil rolling up under it, the thin hiss of metal on metal.

My mother comes into the living room and looks at us. Andrew is reading the TV *Guide*, sequentially, like it was a novel, and I'm spying on the Drapers. Mr Draper is home and I can see he's throwing sofa cushions around. I wonder why a man would come home early from work to do that. I stop and look up at my mum. She has another fish book.

'This is for when you fish-sit.'

'Oh … ya,' I say, 'when is that?' I have no idea
yet what she's talking about.

'I can't remember, but I'll call her and ask.'
There is a sound of something smashing next
door. Mum bends down and looks through the
curtains.

'Maybe I'll wait a while,' she says.

I stare at my mother in disbelief. This is
incredible.

'I have to fish-sit for the Drapers!?!' I yell. But
she's looking at Andrew where he sits, his face
four inches from Thursday night.

'What are you reading, dear?' she asks and
strokes his hair. Without looking up, Andrew
raises the TV *Guide*.

It's night. On top of being a zombie all day, I
can't sleep properly either. I wake up every hour
or so and just seethe with frustration. I look out
with the binoculars but there is never anything to
see. Why can't these people do something
interesting – aren't there neighbourhoods where
people are up all night killing each other?
Tonight, I decide to get up and do something
useful. I read about fish.

They are pitiful pets, really, but I can see why
someone might want a tank in their house; some
of them are lovely. There are Japanese fighting
fish with their long tails, and mutating colours.
Glass catfish that are completely see-through.
Mollies. Tetras. They have sharks the size of a
stick of gum. Hatchetfish with their fat bellies.
Piranhas with under-slung jaws, which can grow
to the size of trash can lids. I gaze at the pictures
of iridescent scales and emotionless eyes and

small snapping mouths. I gaze, half dreaming, at the photos of dissected fish, the mushroom-like frill of gills, the strange little sacks and organs all balled up together. There is a plastic ruler, measuring the wreckage; a white pointer, indicating nothing.

Andrew still won't talk. My mother kisses his hair; my father squats and whispers to him and presses his forehead to Andrew's; nothing works. He comes into my room and we sit together on my bed with our backs against the wall, reading. Neither of us turn a page for half an hour, but our eyes move, wandering over lines of print.

Tuesday, 9 a.m.: excellent. The most excellent things about today are that my mother is calling the movers, and I have the twelve-minute run. Ginger claims she has her period, but the two phys-ed teachers stand in the door to their office, not buying it. They're both huge, spongy and blond, and they wear stop-watches that hang to their groins. One is a man, the other a woman, and no one could ever see the difference between them. Rosalie and I go and get dressed while Ginger begs for her life. She's just going to have to hurry in the end and get dressed like the rest of us. Marty comes in then, her jean vest looking even tighter, and we all stare at her as we struggle into our gym clothes. She strips quickly, and a dozen pairs of eyes gaze openly at her body, knowing she will start last and finish first. With a body like that she could walk through walls. Marty is my friend these days because, as she puts it, I'm a freak like her.

Lilac bushes and mock orange float by on an undulating field of nausea. I feel like I have needles in my lungs. Every time I come out into the sun I feel ten pounds heavier and every time I pass under a tree I feel human again. When it's over I sit in the change room and sleep with my eyes open. As people dress and leave, the two doors swing open, then swing closed and a sliver of the hallway can be seen. Marty is out there waiting for me, smoking.

When I'm ready, we go for fries and gravy. We smoke and eat at the same time, which grosses the waiter out. As usual when I am with Marty, I chatter like an idiot and she listens to me in amused silence. I make up weird facts and theories about things, like that curly hair means your mother didn't get enough sleep; things that would bug Ginger. Marty almost never talks, she gives me room. Marty has failed two years already; she's older than any of my friends and she lives by herself in an apartment. Once in a while her twin brother, who looks nothing like her, pulls into town on his bike and she disappears for a week or two with him.

I grab Marty's cigarette and finish it while she fishes another out of the pack and lights it. No one has seen Marty for quite a while, and she's made no mention of her brother, which is intriguing. When I ask her where she's been lately, she grabs the butt out of my mouth, stubs it out.

'You're tired,' she says, 'go home and sleep.'

But I can't go to sleep. Today is the day I have to go over and meet the Drapers, get instructions about their stupid fish, and my mother has made me promise to thank them for the jam Mrs Draper made. I drag Andrew along for moral

92

support and he follows me like a sleep-walker.
When Mrs Draper meets me at the door her face
jumps out at me, younger than I thought and
more friendly too. I'd stared at that face many
times, but never really seen it clearly. Andrew
stands there in silence and glares at her through
his glasses until she invites us in and takes us
around the house, looking at what she calls 'her
babies'.

There are tanks everywhere, built into walls,
standing in hallways, a big long one that
separates the living room from the dining room,
and all of them have sheets of paper taped to the
glass. On the papers are written instructions, the
names of the species of fish, and pet names with
quote marks around them. 'Dingus.' 'Ralphy.'
'Slow Learner.' In the fridge, they keep a canister
of brine shrimp and lettuce for the shark, Arnie,
and a shallow dish of larvae for the rest of them. I
look at the larvae lying inert beside the parmesan
cheese. I make a mental note to tell my mother
to throw out Mrs Draper's home-made jam.

The husband keeps his distance from me but I
can smell it on him from where I am, like orange
juice that has been left in the sun. Andrew, who
they've tried in vain to butter up, is staring now
at the lists of names, dates, the feeding and saline
instructions like he's committing it to memory. I
have to drag him by the elbow as we go from tank
to tank. I keep looking at Mr Draper and he keeps
looking at his wife with a shallow, wary grin.
She's leaning close to the bright blue tanks and
gazing intently at the fish where they swim in
slow, pointless patterns. Then she tries to show
me a sick crab, which I can't find among all the
greenery and pebbles and toy castles; everything I

look at turns out to be a rock. She tells me that if the crab dies while they are away, I shouldn't blame myself.

A car horn goes off in the driveway and Mr Draper says, 'Jeff.' The woman gets this furious look on her face and hustles us out the door, making me promise to thank my parents for offering my services. Andrew doesn't need to be pushed and is already halfway back into our house. They wave goodbye to us, and wave hello to Jeff, who is coming up the walk. I recognize him; he has red hair, not as thin as I'd thought, and sandals on, and he has a pair of mean blue eyes. I pause on our porch to see Mr Draper give Jeff a long, affectionate bear hug and slap him on the back.

'I think that man is their son,' I say to my mother. She's in the living room, tossing the cat in the air and saying 'Yikes!' over and over. The cat is just as limp as a doll and he's purring.

'What man?'

'The one you thought was having an affair with her,' I say.

'Shh!' she looks absurdly at the wall, 'really?'

'The husband gave him a big hug.'

'Well, they could all three be ... you know ...'

Marty is whistling into the empty hallway. She says the only way to find out is to come right out and ask Mrs Draper. This is typical of Marty, who has the social graces of a snake. I can picture Mrs Draper just standing there, and then fainting. The only sure-fire way is to sick my dad on them, but Dad has opinions about who he will bother pumping for info, and he thinks the Drapers are creepy.

Fish-Sitting

. . . .

'Fish,' he says, 'I hope they move out. Fish is typical of that couple.'

I'm thinking about that, when Mr Butcher comes down the hall and I elbow Marty. She lowers her arm, in which she has a cigarette. A no smoking sign hangs in the cloud over our heads. Marty stands eight inches higher than me so Butcher doesn't see me until he is quite close. The look on his face changes, then, from nervous to blank. 'No smoking, ladies,' he says, as he passes us, and after a second Marty snorts two pencils of smoke from her nostrils.

By the next morning I understand that I'm disappearing again, like a TV signal bizzing into a simple white dot. One minute I'm by the window in G44 with an untouched test in front of me and the sun is coming through and I can see my hands lit up on my lap. The next minute I am in the basement, looking at a pipe. Rosalie grabs my belt loop and drags me to art class. She got bored waiting as I stared at a pair of initials gouged in the drywall next to the pipe. I don't know whose initials they are. Just two people. Maybe it's all over between them, maybe they aren't even in school anymore. I tell Rosalie we should scratch a date in there, 1902, and see if anyone notices. It's exactly the kind of anal little thing that drives her crazy about me. She shoves me into a chair, then crosses the room to get away from me. I watch the art teacher's legs come out of her shorts and her elbows that never straighten.

It's the second night I have to feed the fish, and already I've gotten into the habit of leaving the lights off when I walk through the house. I like the way the blue tanks light everything up and shadows of fish move like clouds over the walls and carpet. The tank lights are on timers and the water is heated, so all I have to do is check the temperature, use the saline meter to make sure the water is salty enough, and give them a tiny amount of food. Fish eat practically nothing. I open the wall units at the top, slide back the grill and drop in a pinch of food. It's a foul-smelling kind of lumpy mess. Some of it floats on the surface and some of it drifts down through the water in clots. When I get up on the chair, the fish go wild and they dart at each other, stab right into the air at my fingers, and shoot from the top of the tank to the bottom, scattering the little blue stones. The crabs tuck in under their shells and the snails sucker themselves tight against the glass, as if a bomb was going off.

Arnie the shark stops moving when I come upstairs and into the hallway, his lidless eye looking at me sideways. He's only as big as my thumb, but I think of him as potentially dangerous. The books say sharks simply refuse to mate in tanks, they'd rather chew each other up. Arnie drifts closer to the glass, staring out at my white T-shirt suspended in the gloomy hall. I drop a lettuce leaf in and he stabs and nips at it. The leaf flips and drifts in the lighted water like a sheet carried away on the wind.

Later, I sit with my feet up on the dining-room table and watch the fish, or spy through the front window with my binoculars. I have a whole different perspective on the neighbourhood from this house – I can see clearly into different rooms. At about nine-thirty, the lady with the cat usually calls someone on the phone. She pulls her hair around and looks at the split ends up close.

Fish-Sitting

. . . .

She points her finger at the air like she's giving an invisible person a lecture. My guess is it's her sister on the phone. I bet there's a lot of fibbing going on, sentences that start with: 'And I told him, I said: Look! ...'

Soon, she hangs up, eats out of a small tub of ice cream and watches TV. Then her cat gets up on the coffee table and licks her toes. It hunches over, looking urgent. I can hardly stand it – I have to get up and scratch my scalp and walk around the room in the dark. I also learn that zit cream boy shaves his armpits. Maybe he's a speed swimmer or something. Maybe not. Then, there's a teenager, who I think is the Bison's daughter. She smokes leaning out her window, stubs the butts out on the shingles and lets them roll into the eaves trough. And downstairs you can see Mrs Bison cutting things up; fish, carrots, sausages, frozen lasagna, hunks of grey meat. Mrs Bison is good with a knife.

But it's all so dull, really. And so, it occurs to me to look around inside the Drapers' house, see if I could find anything incriminating. They have a few sexy books on the shelf above the bed, books with creative suggestions to make sex more fun, but they've kept these next to a medical dictionary with horror-show diagrams and photos. It's a combination guaranteed to put the idea of sex right out of your head. I look in all the drawers, open the bathroom cabinet and inspect all the bottles and clippers and foams. But it's a bleak search. No rubbers or sex devices. No drugs. No embarrassing poems or letters. No medications for anything gross or sad. I spend a long time and come up with nothing.

. . . .

I make my way downstairs in the dark, Arnie whipping back and forth in a panic as I pass, and I grab my binoculars and head for the door. But something stops me. I don't really want to go home at all, these days; I just don't know what to expect when I come in the door – maybe one of them fuming silently, or maybe talking to Andrew, trying to communicate with Mars. I stand in the Drapers' hall and look through the binoculars to our front door. The doorknob appears, big as a pumpkin, motionless and strange. I swing the binoculars round, trees dissolving, colours and shapes blurring and re-forming to the outline of my father.

'Dad,' I say, out loud.

He is standing in the back yard of our house, in the dark, with his hands in his pockets. If I'd never seen this man before in my life, I would have understood him to be what he is: kind, confused, and moving day by day into a future he can no longer elude.

Hippies

I'M SITTING ON THE roof of my house with my legs hanging over the edge. I'm squinting, taking turns putting one running shoe, then the other over the parked cars below. Four roofs over there's an orange cat with a fat head regarding me balefully. I've never seen him before. Maybe he lives up here, eats birds out of the air. He swivels his big head and looks down at the sidewalk where someone is standing.

'Oh my God!' cries a voice.

It's Mrs Baze. She's four foot something, wears funny hats and has badly crossed eyes, one of which she has angled up in my direction. She kind of moves her head around to get me fixed with the other eye, then legs it up the steps and into my house.

'Uh-oh,' I say, 'Mrs Baze and her gaze.' That's one of my mother's.

Our TV aerial creaks in the wind as I lie back and let the sun fall on me. The cat steps away over the gravel and soft tar.

. . . .

Sometimes I come up here at night and look
out at the city, at the twinkling lights and the
cars going down the streets. Planes pass overhead,
invisible except for the flashing lights, the tiny
far-away hiss of engine. Looking up, I can feel the
house sinking under me and the soft black sky
spreading out like something alive.

The best thing is when people go down the
alleyway and I can drop pebbles. They look at the
ground for a while, cogs turning in their heads;
finally, they look up. I have to laugh. I see people
walking along below, swinging their arms. My
father passes down the alleyway with the
lawnmower, and he tells me to cut it out,
without looking up, without stopping.

But Dad doesn't really care. There's the porch
roof one storey down, so why worry? But it's the
worst thing for Mrs Baze. I feed her idea that
young people are basically wild. For example,
she's convinced that hippies congregate in the
park out back of her house and they throw their
empty bottles of hooch over her fence. It might
have happened once, but in her mind, the debris
is always flying – it's a neighbourhood emergency.
The world worries Mrs Baze, and she sees trouble
and inconvenience everywhere. She talks to the
police, the firemen, the hydro guys, door-to-door
salesmen, her vet, any neighbour who stands still
too long. I've seen her in the Safeway, bending
over the bags of sugar, saying: 'This *can't* be the
price!' Boys in red aprons just stamp the goods
and shuffle along the floor away from her; they
keep stamping, keep shuffling.

* * *

'Don't let her catch you again, or I'll kill you,'

my dad says. He and Andrew are scraping at some
pots which got burned during one of our
disastrous dinners. We all try to cook together
now, it's a daily duty. This fact bugs my mother
so much I have to make sure never to mention
food in front of her.

'Why didn't he think of that when I was living
there?' she says.

Dad's unusually pissed off today; maybe it's
the heat. He hacks at a snarl of rock-hard
spaghetti.

'I had to go look at her birds to shut her up,' he
says. 'You wouldn't believe the stink.'

'She should leave injured things alone,' says
Andrew.

Mrs Baze has a knack for being present when
birds get swiped by cars. She takes them to the
vet, sparing no expense to save the dwindling life.
The vet begs and reasons with her, but it does no
good. Once he tried keeping the unconscious
patient overnight for 'observation', putting it
down in secret. But Mrs Baze caught on to that.
Now she follows him into the back room,
watches his every move while the vet keeps up a
vain monologue on 'prolonging the inevitable'.

'I'd change vets,' she told my dad, 'but this one
gives me a discount.' Mrs Baze has an old parrot
which has been with her for ages, and two badly
addled pigeons, Valentine and Bigs. None of them
ever flies farther than from sofa to chair, and Bigs
walks into walls.

* * *

It's Tuesday. A stifling, humid day where the
trees droop and the street seems to fade into
nothing halfway down. Andrew sprays me with

the hose and then I spray him. I hold the dog
down in the mud while Andrew soaks his coat,
and the dog groans under my weight, snapping
irritably at the stream of water. Dad comes
outside, so we go after him, and it doesn't go over
too well. He stomps inside to change his pants.

'Why's he wearing pants in this heat, anyway?'
Andrew says. He and the dog follow Dad in,
trailing water and mud and crushed grass behind
them.

The tap drip-drips against the porch step. The
back gate opens and I turn to look. Nobody's
there, and then my mother is there, her bare feet
sinking into the mud. She's looking down at the
tracks she's making, the perfect marks of toes.
Between two breaths, she's gone, leaving nothing,
no sign.

* * *

Jeannie says she's miserable, she can't sleep in the
heat any better than me. I've called very late, and
now she's reading me stuff as we both lie in bed. I
ask her about my horoscope, she talks to me
about past lives, and birth control and her
mother. Jeannie's Korean and she looks our
birthdays up in her books. My sign keeps
changing; year of the ox, year of the rat.

'This book is crap,' she says and I hear a clatter
in the background as the book falls to her
bedroom floor. We ignore the clicks and sighing
as my father checks the line, checks the line.

* * *

My dad stands in the bathroom scrutinizing his
own sour expression in the mirror. He is wearing
a tuxedo with the dust of years on it. Today is
Castor and Netty's twenty-fifth wedding

anniversary and my father will go, alone, out to the car and drive the fifteen miles to the Silver Birch Golf Club which Castor has booked for the evening.

While Dad's gone, Andrew and I filch a beer each. Andrew strikes one match after another until two packs are gone, then flushes them all down the toilet.

Dad comes home very late. He slumps at the dining-room table with his tie dangling, taps his finger on the wood, scratches a little light spot. I bring him a beer and he thanks me, but doesn't touch it.

'How many people,' he says, 'can say they fit into a twenty-year-old tuxedo?' He holds out his arms in a weary gesture which is totally without pride. Jeannie says my dad is a babe; so's my mum. Too bad about me. His clear blue eyes, his tanned hand tapping again at the table.

* * *

'They're still just lying there,' I say. I'm up on the roof, watching the couple across the street do nothing in their bedroom. Jeannie is with me, but she prefers to stay back, close to the attic window.

'Okay,' Jeannie's voice says, 'did you know that in mythology the crow is symbolic of death during sex, you know, like old men who take young wives and have a heart attack?'

'Get out. Really?'

'Naw. But it sounds good, doesn't it?'

Way to the east, you can see the light of a train passing along the uneven walls of warehouses. The sky is silky and black and it seems like the

air isn't moving anywhere on earth. Jeannie shifts
uncomfortably. She doesn't like heights. Also, I
know she doesn't see much point in sitting up on
a roof. She sighs and flicks a pebble at me.

'What are they doing *now*?'

* * *

I'm trying to sleep, relaxing my toes, then my
ankles. Fat lot of good it does. Two guys on our
street are playing *Miami Vice*, squealing around
corners in the middle of the night like dogs
chasing each other in circles. I've moved my bed
under the window so I can look up into the
branches of the trees. I remember my feet
dangling down from the roof. Headlights pan
across my ceiling, attended by a howl of tires.
They make several passes and then, finally, don't
come around anymore. It is quiet, dark. I gaze up
into the tree, and for a moment I think I can hear
the leaves chattering to themselves in grieved
little voices.

In my dreams I venture forward into the dark,
putting my feet carefully between sharp
flagstones. A brutal light keeps blaring on and off
– it is hard to see where to walk. I look down to
see a crow in the gutter, caught under something
wet and mossy, its sleek, muscled neck writhing
in its attempts to pull free. I grab at the dark mass
and discover that it is made of pine needles, resin,
clay – a gluey weight that clings to the bird's body
as if feeding there. I hear my mother's voice,
sharp in my ear, saying: '*Nothing* is worth that.' I
wake up quick, blindly identifying my body's
angle across the bed, acknowledging the
ambulance light that flashes in the air above me.

* * *

Hippies

It's the morning and the dog is hopping up and whistling in his throat. Mrs Baze's parrot sits in his cage on our fridge, angles his head and examines, with one disc eye, the questionable business below. We don't know the parrot's name, yet. Valentine and Bigs have gone to another family, one without a cat or dog. Last night, the neighbours who gathered to help outside Mrs Baze's house decided that our dog was gentle enough, and the parrot looked tough enough, and so we got him.

Mrs Baze's heart medicine made her retain water, she kept fainting in her house, finally staggering out onto a neighbour's lawn where she fell down, jabbering in her nightie. She calls hourly from the hospital and asks us to put the phone up to 'Florio's' cage for her to shout to him. The bird bites his toenails and opens his mouth to show his dry little stump of a tongue. Andrew puts a stick in the cage and Florio snaps it in half with one lightning-fast strike.

* * *

'They took three bags out of me,' Mrs Baze says, pouring me another cup of grainy tea, 'They put this tube up my ... *you know*, and it stretched me out. I still have to wear pads.' She sits down with a heartfelt sigh in her chair and looks out over her garden. I, too, take in the willow tree, the ivy-burdened fence. There are flowers growing in rows and clumps, bordering the lawn and hanging out of windows, petals staining the patio bricks. Some are lush and thick-stalked, others bent as if by fatigue. Still others peek from doorways like consumptives, pale, with shrivelled stalks and leaves chewed to shreds by cats.

'You sure have a green thumb, Mrs ...' I begin
to say, just as a beer bottle comes whiffling over
the ivy-covered fence and lands with a clink on
the grass. It's our brand.

'There!' Mrs Baze cries, triumphantly. She
fixes me with that bizarre gaze.

'*You're* my witness!'

This is the moment Mrs Baze has been waiting
for. She is electrified, up out of her seat; shaking
her little fists over the cookies and fussy, chipped
tea cups; shouting abuse at the air. The parrot
stands on his cage, tethered by the ankle, flapping
his wings as if to mock her.

'Oh!' says Mrs Baze, just like someone hit her,
'Oh!' I reach out to hold down the rattling plates.
I blow tufts of dry feather away from my tea.

Somewhere beyond the flowers and ivy and
leaning-over trees, in the soft, running footfalls of
the retreating bottle-thrower, I can hear my
brother's low giggle.

Boomerang

MY MOTHER DECIDES TO make me remember
Mr Whitnell. Her memory is perfect and she has
always felt I was underprivileged because I could
never remember anything. At least, I can't
remember anything in its right order, and I rarely
know if it's a real memory or just something I
heard somewhere. If you have a mother like
mine, your own memories become unnecessary.

I go to her house in the late afternoons
sometimes and she gives me a cup of her jitter-
producing coffee. Lately, she's been working on
my childhood memories, prodding me, bringing
up traumas and excitements I only dimly
recognize as having happened to me. It's my
mother versus the fog in my head.

Today's subject is Mr Whitnell who used to
live on our street and, as my mother puts it, used
to go 'screaming around at night'. He lived six
doors down from us in a small blue-and-green
bungalow. He had some disease of old age, or
perhaps the problem was latent in him all his life.
One way or the other, there would be sounds of a
disturbance in that house, things breaking, his

sister shouting his name over and over like a parrot.

'And then, crash!' my mother says, 'out he runs, all over the street, howling. Are you telling me you don't remember this?'

I say I don't and she regards me silently for a moment.

'You're not so good on things previous to last week, are you?' she says.

I admit for the four-hundredth time that I'm not. I remember last week in Technicolor, but that'll fade, soon enough. I do remember bits of childhood, like hating every square second of school, especially recess when I was supposed to go out and have 'fun' with people I didn't know. There were dogs and cats I felt closer to than most of the girls at school. I remember the seasons going by. I remember a dentist coming to do a talk. He had a huge plastic tooth and an even bigger red toothbrush and I remember him dropping the tooth on the floor by mistake.

'Well, look at that!' he said, trying to cover up, 'See how strong teeth are?'

And I remember summer in my neighbourhood, the trees crowding over the sidewalks, maple keys sticking to my shoes, the sidewalk, the windshields of parked cars in the morning. Everyone seemed to have kids at the same time – they were all my age. After a while, people had more kids, and those were all the same age as my brother. I don't suppose it could really have been like that, but it seems that way in my mind, still.

Boomerang

My dad has a boomerang, a real one, and it sits
up on the mantelpiece, kind of leaning sideways,
like someone has just come in from killing
kangaroos and left it there. He also used to make
rough ones from plywood, and he'd teach any kid
who wanted to know how to throw it. He'd go out
to the park, kids holding onto his pants pockets
and his hands, and he would whip the boomerang
into the air and watch it swoop up. A moment
later, my dad and eight kids would hit the deck as
the boomerang snapped back over their heads. I
only saw him actually catch it once, a single
beautiful moment when he reached up and it
came back to him. But usually, he and his short
entourage would have to fetch it from where it
had embedded itself in the grass like a javelin.

People called on my father, for various reasons,
all the time. Broken lawnmower blades, flooded
garages, even bread recipes. I do remember an old
lady coming over and begging my father to come
over to her house. She was angry or frightened, it
was hard to tell. When I ask my mother about
that time, she knows right away what it was.

'That's when he faked being dead. His sister
called your father over, pretending to be in a
panic, but all she wanted was to embarrass the
old man. He was there on the couch, holding his
breath like a child. There, see? You do remember
him,' she says.

Again, I have to say no. All I remember is the
blue and green front door, half open, the windows
with their gauzy curtains, and the few waxy
tulips that drooped off the porch.

Next door to the Whitnells was a dog that
howled and howled, like a madness had come

over it. The young couple in that house kept getting dogs for their little girl, and the dogs kept getting loose and disappearing. They called two of them by the same name because she got so upset about the first one getting away. But the two dogs looked nothing alike; perhaps the name was enough to calm her. My father sawed a big stake for them and hammered it deep into their lawn and attached the dog to it by a long thick rope. The man thanked him and tried not to look hostile. Nevertheless, they used the stake, and that dog stayed. It was a good idea, but it didn't seem a dog could lead a normal life in that house. The little girl ceased to give a shit about pets, and every day the dog would go round and round the stake until his cheek touched it.

'I've been having dreams about your father,' my mother tells me, 'and, in one of them, we're supposed to get married. The church is right there across the street, and your father is in his coveralls, those blue things, and he is wiping the ceiling. I ask him "Why aren't you dressed? They're all waiting for us!" and he looks down at me like I'm crazy.'

She slaps the table and looks at me. 'I should have known about that man.'

I tell her it was just a dream, she shouldn't get so worked up. But I, too, have seen my father on tables, on ladders, on two stacked chairs, wiping the ceiling before company comes over. He takes off his dress shoes, removes dishes and cutlery from the already set table, and fiddles with the overhead light, or removes cobwebs. My visual memory of this is my dad, up on a chair, forehead beaded with sweat, turning as the doorbell rings. I

tell my mother, however, that her dream was just
a dream, not a message.

Dad's still living there and Mum has a place of
her own. They're both different now, fewer ups
and downs. I occupy a difficult space between
them. I go to school, hang out with my friends
and wonder which one of my parents will go off
in me some day, like a time-bomb. If I could
choose, I don't know what my choice would be.
Dad marches around after dinner, starting three
projects at once, and then falls asleep on the
couch having finished none of them. In the
meantime, without ever seeming to sit down and
do it, he's managed to carefully mark a pillow-
sized stack of students' papers. He remembers
every student he's ever had – the city is littered
with them now – but he doesn't remember any of
their names. He has trouble, sometimes,
remembering mine, and he runs through the
family names one by one till he gets to me.

My mother, on the other hand, has a trick: she
says 'Give me a word, any word at all, and I can
think of a song with that word in it.' She's even
called me at night and said 'I've got it! It's a little
song about a hardware store, and in it is the word
grommet.' She remembers all the words and sings
the whole song through.

When I was younger and my parents were still
together, some older boys hung Mark Wilson up
on a fence by his underwear. Mark was a little
bastard, but it hurt and embarrassed him, and he
hung there for a while before some of us found
him. Most of his clothes were on the grass, far
beneath his kicking feet. We weren't tall enough
to reach him, so we ran to my house and got my

dad. When my mum asked what was up, we all pretended it was nothing. She just stood there and watched us rush my father off to the park, dragging him by his fingers. Dad lifted Mark down and he immediately ran away, crying and holding his clothes against himself.

In many ways, I'm a morbid person, ready to think the worst of people. I wonder if a little thing like that – like a boy's humiliation – stays with a person and changes them in little ways. I always read the back pages of the newspaper first, all the mayhem and blood. I skim through encyclopaedias of murderers and it seems that each one had a little trauma, or a strange childhood, or something in them that grew, like a bad seed. I read these books at bedtime and then have dreams where I get shot and my last thought is always 'Oh, shit!'

Mark Wilson is grown now and has gone to Thailand. My mother believes he went to join a cult, my bet is he's a Buddhist. My father doesn't remember him, doesn't remember pulling a boy in his underwear off any fence. Dad's almost as bad as I am. I come reeling home from Mum's sometimes, drunk on my own history, and try it all out on him. But there's no way – he's almost as bad as I am. Say, for instance, that the neighbours down the street returned a belt sander or an extension cord – my dad would hold it in his hand like an unexpected gift.

'Is this mine?' he says.

'Okay,' my mother says, 'remember when your best friend, what's her name, moved away and you spent a summer with nothing to do and I wanted to strangle you?'

· ·

I do remember this; I remember the girl's letters being perplexing, like they were written by a person in grade three. I remember being frustrated and bored and yelling at my mother, her face blooming with anger. Later I was sitting in the bath crying, a common event that summer, and the window was open with the cool air coming in. I stood up and sobbed onto the window sill, splashing my feet. Just then, Mr Whitnell shuffled by out on the sidewalk. He was in his slippers, with no pyjama top on. I watched his skinny body slide by, his scrawny chest raw as a plucked capon. He was hissing. I expected to see someone else running after him, but no one came. There were little smacking sounds, like he was hitting a lamp post with a stick. Then Mr Whitnell shuffled and hissed back the other way.

'I knew you'd remember him if you tried,' my mother says. 'Some time around then, he lost his voice and got much worse, so they took him away. Poor old thing; his sister just gave up on him. That's the way it is with relationships.'

Mum is satisfied, but I still can't picture his face. It's like these are stories I heard and only imagined I was there. The whole thing disturbs me sometimes. I feel like I might be an alien dropped here in this family, while the real me, along with all my memories, is somewhere else, lost.

I go home that night and sit there with my dad, our feet up on the coffee table, watching TV until the test-pattern with the Indian chief comes on. My dad has been asleep since he put his feet up, and I'm lying there like a zombie. I elbow him and say 'It's tomorrow already, Dad.' He erupts from the couch, his sweater crooked, and staggers towards the stairs, his arms out in front in case he bumps something.

'Dad?' I say, as he creaks up to the second floor, 'do you remember Mr Whitnell? That old man down the street?'

'Who ...?' he rubs his face.

'Mr Whitnell. Remember?'

'Oh God,' he says, 'he fed you so much candy once you puked all day. We never told your mother how that one happened.' I want to ask him more but he's already gone, hustling up there to hog the bathroom. Tomorrow, I think, I'll ask him tomorrow, and I close my eyes. The test pattern is still glowing in the dark inside my head.

I imagine myself sitting on the back steps with Mr Whitnell, and there's a bunch of chocolate bars lined up. He's saying: six plus three? and I'm saying: eleven. He's laughing and saying: try again, separating them into two bunches. Six and three? Before lunchtime we finish them all, even though he's diabetic, even though his sister is in the sun room, snoring, perhaps dreaming of being free. I can see his face perfectly, and the trees beyond, and the crooked back fence. Mr Whitnell is a cute old guy, with nearly crossed eyes. My dad appears at the door, and me and Mr Whitnell look up to greet him, our faces and fingers sticky with chocolate. My dad gets all these different expressions on his face, one after the other, a string of veiled and unhappy thoughts.

I don't know what happens next. My neck hurts from sitting on the couch too long. I shift a bit, and soon I'm asleep. It's Utah this time, and I'm driving, and everything is truly bizarre.

The Electric Curtain

I'M IN A DISGUSTING mood that morning,
sitting in a shaft of sunlight and thinking about
Nick for the first time in a long time. To keep
busy, I look for my brother in the paper, folding
the pages out over my toast and coffee, but I can't
find the right section. It's a community
newspaper, with print that stinks like cigars.

So far, everything's about our neighbourhood's
pitiful blues festival – a disaster that goes on for a
week – you can listen all day and never hear a
single blues tune. Some days, you stand on your
porch and sounds of the various bands drift
together, playing 'The Girl From Ipanema' or
'Bad, Bad, Leroy Brown'. The mess goes on all day
and into the night, tunes coming through the
bedroom window, forcing me to cover my head
with a pillow. I wake up humming songs I hate.
The newspaper chirps at me: 'This Thursday!'

For some reason, I woke up this morning
thinking Nick was going to buy our house. I
struggled out of bed to warn Dad, and was
halfway down the stairs when I realized it
couldn't be true. I sat on the bottom step then,

and held my head and tried to convince myself
that I wasn't on my way into another Nick-
fixation. Nonetheless, the carpet under my feet
didn't seem to belong to me anymore. I was a bit
worried, because things had been going well, for
so many months.

I finally find Andrew in the 'Home on the
Range' section. It's the kitchen section, but some
weeks they run out of food tips and type-riddled
recipes, and they throw in anything that might
have happened near a kitchen – or for that matter,
anywhere indoors. Today, it's Andrew's solar-
powered curtains.

'Look,' I say, as Andrew digs around under the
sink, 'It's about your curtains.'
'Huh,' says Andrew.
'They call you a genius – actually they call you
a *gerius* – and it says that solar energy ...'
'Those curtains don't work. They're crap,' he
says. This is his opinion of almost everything he
does, and I've given up telling him not to be so
down on himself. I'm looking at a grainy picture
of my brother's face. He is intent, serious, holding
up a little solar chip.
'You look like a grown man, here, Andrew,' I
say, holding the paper out.
'I am a grown man,' he says.

It's true; he's seventeen years old, six foot two
with arms like a boxer's. If he keeps growing at
this rate, he'll soon be able to pick Dad up and
bounce him on his knee.

My brother yanks a long string of nylon rope
out from under the sink and inspects the frayed
ends. He goes out of the room, leaving the

cupboard door open and dragging the rope behind
him. The dog stares at the twitching, frayed tail
as it rounds the corner, but he doesn't rise to
chase it.

In many ways, my brother is an updated
version of my father. Between the two of them,
they have booby-trapped the whole house.
Everywhere, there are devices which have been
strung up, tied together, rigged with electrical
tape and timers and light-emitting diodes and
beepers. Apart from the curtains, which I know
are Andrew's, I'm not sure which project belongs
to whom, and anyway, they collaborate on things.
My father has a coffee-maker on his bedside table
that turns on when his alarm goes off. The
problem is that, if he turns the alarm off, the
coffee stops brewing. Every morning, my father
leaps up and heads for the bathroom while his
clock *raaangs* away under a pillow.

The doorbell plays Christmas music, the
garbage bin is booby-trapped against the dog, as
well as raccoons, and Dad's car gets really good
mileage. My father is in heaven, having finally
convinced somebody that life without gadgets is
no life at all. Even my mother has softened and
allowed Andrew to do a few things around her
house, though she keeps asking for the doorbell
to be changed to something other than 'Silent
Night'.

During the day I work for an optometrist who
calls me 'sweetie', and who very obviously
loathes her job. At night I come home, drink beer
and write my ridiculous poems. Occasionally, I
write something that makes sense, but mostly
they are about lizards and apes and the A-bomb,

which is why I'll never get famous. I can't seem to write about normal things, like, say, the optometrist and her fancy shoes and the crying sessions I hear from inside her little darkened room. She thinks I can't hear her, but I can hear spiders walking, and now I know all about my boss, about her fondness for white powder, and her less-than-happy relationship with Revenue Canada.

In fact, it was during one of her crying jags that I met Nick. If I was more like my mother, I would have considered that, in itself, to be a bad sign. I came out of the office door almost at a run, with mail under my arm, hoping she would be finished weeping by the time I got back. I passed a workman who was repairing the marble by the elevator doors. He was bent over, so all I saw was his long back, and his butt. Later, coming back the other way, I smiled broadly at him as I passed, and he swivelled on his heel to watch me go.

Over the week we began taking time to visit with each other. I'd stand with him, leaving the office door open so I could get to the phone quickly, or else he'd sit on his toolbox beside my desk and drink coffee. On his last day, I asked him out to dinner. He looked like the question had caught him off guard and he stammered a series of little nothings. For a moment I thought I'd made an error in judgement – he didn't like me; he didn't like girls; he was gay. But then Nick stammered that he'd like very much to go out, and he shoved his hands in his pockets, leaned forward, and kissed me on the cheek.

The next night we were sitting in a cramped little restaurant where they hang the bread basket

on a rope over the table. Almost right away he
told me he had a girlfriend, and he was feeling
guilty. I stared at him. I asked him why he had
come, then, and he said because he'd wanted to,
but he was confused. By then, we were both
confused and neither of us could eat anything. I
picked at my food and so did he. We sat there
trying to smile, or talk. After a long depressing
interval, we paid and left the restaurant.

In the municipal parking lot where he had
parked was a gang of little boys and they chased
each other like puppies and struck out at tires
and bumpers with their sticks. Nick was going
home, and I was going home, and I knew he
wouldn't offer me a ride.
'Well, thanks,' I said.
He leaned over and kissed me on the cheek
again. I should have turned and walked away, but
I stood there like a fool, waiting. Then he started
doing it again, in earnest this time, pressing his
groin and thighs hard against me. It was
absolutely great. After a little time, we became
aware of kissing noises from the shadows, and so
we hurried away down darkened streets to a place
by the water. We stood stupidly staring at a
warehouse. The wind blew on my face and I
closed my eyes against the airborne grit. Nick
said he thought he should be going.

We had this superb fight about why we were
there together and who had started it. By the time
we left each other – both furious and dazed –
Nick had unbuttoned my shirt, pulled my skirt
up, I'd had both hands down his pants, and we'd
shouted at each other twice about who was being
manipulative. It was amazing. Later, slumped
alone in the back of a taxi, I felt like I'd been

sitting, utterly drunk in a movie theatre, my whole life.

Of course, he called me at work a week later. We saw each other secretly, irregularly. The sex was honest, but not unusual. At work, I'd whisper into the phone to him while patients dozed in the waiting room. This went on until he felt compelled to tell his girlfriend. Then it was all over – for two weeks.

I was sitting reading on the back porch when the phone rang and it was Nick on the other end. I went straight over to his apartment and had frankly superb sex, the kind that, in retrospect, gives you a little shock that it actually happened to you. In the kitchen afterwards, he kept looking nervously at the clock on the stove, and I figured it was time for me to go.

I confessed to Andrew about all this; I tell him about most things, and he followed the story attentively. But when it was over he shook his head.
'What happened to the guy with the beard?' he asked. 'I liked that one.' I looked at him, unable to remember, at that moment, who he was talking about.

The weeks droned on and I didn't hear from Nick again. My friend Jeannie told me: 'You should be proud of yourself for surviving him,' but she also said: 'If you ever find yourself being cheated on, you'll know you deserve it.' In private moments, I found myself rehearsing confrontations with him until, over the months, my accusations became like mantras, then the words meant nothing, then I forgot he existed.

The Electric Curtain

Sitting in the silent office, with the rack of ugly frames and files and order forms and past due bills, I gaze at the closed door and listen to the elevators as they hum up and down beyond. A patient, who is late for her appointment, crashes through the door, knocking over the coffee table and a half-dead plant.

'Made it!' she barks, her lenses fogging into blind discs, and just then I hear a tremulous sigh from the examination room behind me, and the snap of the lights being turned on.

It's official now, I want another job.

When I get home, my grandparents' Cadillac is parked half on the driveway, half on the lawn, and steam is coming out of the bathroom window upstairs. The keys are still in the ignition, but the car is empty. Andrew is in the garage leaning over his motorcycle and a girl is standing next to him, smoking. She keeps on asking him what he's doing *now*, and he keeps telling her to put the cigarette out.

I've seen the girl annoying Andrew before, she's the daughter of the Bison, the ugly man across the street, and everyone agrees that it's lucky she doesn't look like him. She's about fifteen and pretty, a hint of a widow's peak on her forehead, a mouth like a poppy. One evening, she even stuck around so long we had to ask her to have dinner with us. She and my father had a great time discussing her parents' peculiar marriage. For instance, the Bison tells his wife when he's on the verge of having an affair and begs her to go and talk the other woman out of it. My father finds it all quite demented. During all of this, Andrew was looking at me like it was my job to get rid of her.

I go inside and stand in the hall listening. Someone is having a bath and I conclude it's my grandfather. I creep over and look at the calendar, but there is nothing there to indicate that Dad is expecting them. My grandmother comes rushing out of the front room, thrilled.

'The curtains are electric!' she says as she passes.

'What are you doing here, Granny?' I ask, but she's gone upstairs to tell her husband about the boy's latest invention.

My grandparents don't remember names. I think that's why they gave their sons such odd names; Castor, Bishop and North; names that don't exactly blend in. I have been called 'Becky', 'Annabel', even 'Tony', whatever comes to mind. My brother, generally, is 'the boy'.

My grandfather comes down the stairs in a towel, trailed by my grandmother. He ignores me and goes into the front room where he stands brazen in the window and puts his hand over the solar chip. The curtains, thinking it's nighttime, slowly draw closed.

'There!' my grandmother crows, 'You see?'

He takes his hand away and the curtains squeak open again. He does this a few more times until the mechanism makes a low hum and finally seizes, halfway closed. We all scatter, hoping Andrew saw nothing.

I've got music on in my room and I'm lying on the floor, smoking a cigarette. Me and my boss started smoking around the same time and, for some reason, we still hide it from each other.

'Want some coffee, sweetie?' she says, her hand already on the knob.

'No, no!' I cry, 'I'll get it,' but she's out the door and I sit back, glaring at her retreating lab coat. She gets to smoke, and I don't, and we both know she owes me one.

I watch the smoke curl toward the ceiling. The music stops and an ad for the blues festival comes on, awful oom-pa-pa in the background. I sit up, infuriated: oom-pa-pa!? Why call it a blues festival at all? A woman's voice purrs that there's only two days to go, admission is free, and then she names a bunch of bands with stupid names. Jim Dandy. Fred Moodie and the Mississauga Mood Mix. My favourite is a couple of idiot guys called the Two Tones. I whack the clock radio off, put my cigarette out, and stamp downstairs.

I find Andrew at the dining-room table wiping the grease from his hands with a yellow cloth. Grandfather is still swishing around in the bath, humming. I figure he said something mean to my grandmother again, because she has taken off in the car, leaving a long streak of burnt rubber on the street outside. I can picture him up there, reading a magazine, unperturbed.

'How's it going?' I say.

'I should have bought the Honda. This machine wastes oil.' I'm so irritable, I feel like I might cry.

'Andrew,' I begin, but my voice drops off and I don't really know what I was going to say anyway. He glances up at me, his face alert. He's a good-looking young man, and I can see why the girl pursues him. He's not stupid, either, because he gets up, then, comes around the table and hugs me and thumps my back. After a while, he sits back down and takes up the oily cloth again.

'Andrew, why don't you like that girl? She's pretty, isn't she?'
'Yes, she is.'
'She likes you, right?'
'She likes me, but she's fifteen years old.'
'So what? You're only seventeen.'
'Fifteen is young; that girl hasn't even got all her teeth yet. That's a fact. You get your last teeth when you're twenty-one.'

I'm considering my brother, and thinking: do I have some kind of problem seeing the impossible for what it is? There was this time in high school I went on a diet, just because of Maria's brother. I wouldn't eat Christmas dinner, sat with a plate of dry toast in front of me, until my mother couldn't stand it anymore and asked me to leave the table. I went down a waist size, got a lot of colds, and it was all for nothing. To Maria's brother, I was just another little girl, all of us squealing away up in Maria's room, no better than a box of puppies.

Sex isn't the problem. I don't seem to have any trouble with sex, and most of my boyfriends are nice people – the guy with the beard, the law student, the petty criminal, the wine-expert, the guy with the truck. I liked them all fine. But once in a while, I pick some guy and lose my mind over him. Maybe it's the poetry; maybe it's got some kind of side-effect.

Dad comes through the door, dropping his

briefcase, bags of groceries, and a new leash for the dog, since the last leash got buried.

'What happened to Andrew's curtains?' he asks. From above, there is the unmistakable sound of someone's backside squeaking around in the tub. Dad looks at Andrew, looks at me, looks at the ceiling, and then curses, swearing his way into the kitchen.

* * *

It is a cool, damp night and the dog hops around in the dark backyard, woofing at a squirrel. The squirrel tightrope-walks along a telephone line, past the upstairs windows, and then disappears into the blackness of a tree. Sitting outside on a garden chair, I listen to the sounds of rotten blues bands warming up several blocks over. By the end of a week of this music, I will feel like I've been rubbed with a hairbrush. Tonight, I make a bet with myself that the first tune I hear will be something from *Cats*. To my surprise, the sounds form themselves into a giddy, tumbling version of 'Trouble in Mind'. I stand up, intrigued, and walk out the back gate to see what's going on. My dad and Andrew have escaped already, and my grandparents are asleep in front of the TV, where a cooking lady chatters soundlessly.

People stream along the sidewalk, often being forced out onto the road. Streetcars inch carefully through the crowd, empty and inviting. Most restaurants have a band glittering in the front window, under temporary lights. Some bands are arranged on the sidewalk, while several battle each other in the park, electrical cords running everywhere and light stands wavering in the crowd. I know from experience that, later on in

the evening, there will be a few drunken scuffles,
people swinging punches at empty air, cars
burning rubber up and down the streets. I am
looking around for my father or my brother, but
instead, under a woozy string of lanterns, I see
Nick.

I think: great, perfect, fucking hell, but I find
myself walking towards him through the crowd.
He sees me coming and turns to escape. A
woman next to him grabs at his shirt, the way
one grabs at a child who runs too much, but she
misses him, shrugs, goes on talking to her friends.

I follow Nick around the corner and down a
side street which is dark from the overhang of
trees. Cars line the curb and people's fences lean
out over the sidewalk. It is quiet, there, and the
air is damp. I am running on high, staring at his
perfect, fascinating, panicked face.

'Don't you ever think about me?' I say,
advancing on him.
'This isn't good ...'
'Answer me.'
He gawps at me, mouth unhinged. I get closer,
and he doesn't bother backing away. He seems to
be calculating something.
'Do you ever think about me?' I say, softer.
'Yes,' he admits, reddening.
'What do you think about?'
'You know, just....'

He's cornered, squirming in the shadows, and I
am about to have a heart attack, my pulse out of
control. We both just stand there, stunned and
waiting.

· ·

'Remember the time in the truck?' I say, 'Do you remember what you said?'

He aims a furtive look over my shoulder to the light of the street.

'I miss you sometimes,' he murmurs.

'There! You see?'

'What?'

'You're so maddening. I can make you admit things that aren't true.'

'Look, I don't know …'

'I bet I can make you want me again.'

'I'm leaving now,' he announces, but he doesn't move.

'Sure, go ahead. You'll go home tonight and you won't tell your girlfriend anything about this. And you'll wish you'd taken the chance to kiss me again – no one's looking, no one would know. You'll sit there over breakfast and wish you had.'

He grabs me, then, on cue, and kisses me. We both look back at the street and then shuffle into the shadow of a parked van where we can do it some more, pulling vainly at shirts and belts. Distantly, the sound of people's voices come to us, a small warning, coming closer, then drifting away again.

Nick stands back to rub his face.

'Can we just wait a second, here,' he says, indicating his pants, adjusting himself cautiously, 'I have to wait.' He leans on the van and watches me while I fix my clothes. It's a remote, disturbing gaze. I know, with certainty, that I can look forward to another couple of months of mental illness. A car goes by and Nick seems to awaken as the lights sweep his face.

'I have to go,' he says.

'And I just have to do this one thing before you

do,' I reply, and I slap him hard. It's done before I know what I'm doing. He gives me a simple, mean look, but he almost seems pleased. I watch him walk away, back to the light and noise, his hands stuffed into his pockets, his cheek burning.

By the time I get back, all the lights in the house are off, except for the oven light which glows yellow as I retrieve a beer from the fridge and a frozen cigarette from the icebox. I see the next few months spread out before me like a puddle and there's nothing I can do about it. I just have to wait for everything to come back to normal again.

The new dog pads in and slumps heavily on my feet, forcing me to yank them free. I have no idea why he does this. He came to us about a year ago, after my mother left. Perhaps it was my state of mind then, but I never expected him to stay. He still has a collar around his neck that says he belongs to someone else, someone who moved or at least changed their telephone number. We haven't even named him, just call him Dog, and it doesn't seem to matter to him.

Sometimes, I worry about running into his real owner while I'm walking him. It's a scene that I often imagine in detail: a man hurrying across the street, calling out, the dog pulling on the leash, barking. There will be a warm reunion, followed by an awkward moment, the dog confused, wagging, the dog belonging, for an instant, to no one. Then, the real owner smiles, his hand extended to take the leash. I see myself giving the dog back; I imagine the man thanking me.

. . . .

Sometimes, thinking about this, I panic in the middle of a walk and turn back home, hustling the dog past all the smells that clamour for his attention – trees, fences, garbage cans, the hubcaps of cars. I feel that the only thing keeping him with me is the leash. But the dog shows no real sign of leaving. The front door of our house is usually open all day and, when I feel uneasy, I can go and see him out on the driveway, not moving, sleeping in a patch of shade, the sun falling down, and nothing changed.

The Funeral

FOR SOME REASON, I've entered a period in my
life where I strike like a cobra. The kitchen boy
doesn't even speak English, standing there, red-
faced, by the open back door, a cigarette dangling
from his hand, but he knows what I'm suggesting.
Christmas Eve is tomorrow and I can smell them
cooking things in preparation. I haven't figured
out the logistics of what I'm pursuing, and before
I can, I spot my dad and realize it's time to duck
down a hallway, perhaps come back later to work
things out.

There are lances hanging from the walls and
dark red tapestries and chairs too stiff to be sat
on. Hung along the halls are paintings of horses
that look like overripe fruit, great huge rumps,
tiny little hooves. The walls are stone, the floors
are stone with carpets running everywhere, and
the lobby is full of stained glass.

'This is crazy,' my mother says, but she
sounds thrilled, 'insane expense.' Bishop says it
reminds him of horror movies. We all stand
around, with our luggage at our feet, looking at
the tourists who come and go, the mounted heads
of game animals, the chandelier, the runner

carpets snaking away into dark hallways. Castor
seems happy now. Now we're all together.

We're at a hotel in the mountains where
everyone speaks different languages, four
adjoining rooms in the old wing; my father and
brother together, Castor and Netty, Mum and me
together and Bishop with his most recent woman,
who looks to be quite a bit overweight: Auntie
Merry. My grandparents can't come because
they're not talking to each other again.

It was my uncle Castor's idea. He owns the
hotel, or part-owns it, or something. No one
really knows where Castor gets his money or
what he does with it. Whatever the case is, all the
staff know who he is, they murmur at him in
various languages, he knows his way through the
staff hallways, and he gets memos and all his
mail brought to him. It was also his idea to invite
my mother, who arrived with a small yellow bag,
took one look at my father – whom she hadn't
expected – looked back at Castor and said a word
I'd never heard her use before. My father looked
stricken. Castor threw his hands down in disgust
and wondered out loud why he even bothered.

We're all together for the first Christmas since
anyone knows, and right off, we hear someone
has died. My dad always hears about things first,
but even he's not clear on whose funeral it is. My
mother, who doesn't know why she's come here
at all, isn't surprised.
'Typical of this family,' she says, 'we're all
going to a funeral, but we don't know whose.'

The hotel is jammed with people. A woman
passes me wearing the largest fur I have ever

seen, drifts close to the bellboy, and kicks him as
she passes. From the bellboy's dull glare, I can see
she does this a lot. My father is all over the hotel,
talking to people and finding out as much about
things as he can. He speaks passable German and
French. He finds out what people do for a living,
how much they make and why they've come here
to the hotel. I see him by the huge front doors,
working on a fat man from some place where
they like suede a lot.

'Any idea who died?' I ask my uncle. He's
sitting on the pool table reading a European
royalty magazine. His face says he's never seen
anything so disgusting.

'Parasites,' he blusters, 'breeding and sleeping
in late and sipping brandy.' He's got a drink next
to him on the felt and it looks like brandy.

'Look at this so-called man,' he says, 'look at
the state of him. His head must weigh fifty
pounds.' He marches off in disgust to show my
father. As soon as he's gone, I guzzle what's left of
his drink.

* * *

I've managed to convince the kitchen boy to
come up to my room. I have him on the bed and I
am lying on him. He's laughing and trying to
unbutton his white uniform. I jump up and pull
the tall heavy curtains closed and the room is
sunk in darkness, so that when I go back to the
bed I have to be careful not to knee or elbow him.
I'm hoping my mother, who shares my room with
me, doesn't come in. But she's downstairs with
the rest of them in the lounge. That's where I
was, until I spotted the kitchen boy, wandering
down the hall with his paper crown.

Later, the kitchen boy, whose name is Hans, shows me a back stairway the staff uses. There is a big sign in four languages saying an alarm will sound, but he pushes the door open and shows me where the wires have been grounded on an overhead pipe. We sit in the stairwell and he teaches me the German words for all kinds of body parts, and before too long, I begin to wish he'd go away. My mind drifts off to a young man I saw earlier, standing by the concierge, looking lost.

* * *

'Dad,' I start, dodging the people coming in the front door, 'Dad, do I have to go to this funeral? I might not feel well. Maybe it's better if I stay in my room, read a book ...' I trail off.

He's looking over my head.
'Hmm?' he says, giving me the bag of wrapped presents he's carrying. I watch him wander off to sit with my mother. To a stranger, my parents would look just like any married couple. Their looks are similar; they have the same lilt to their voice, the same upright way of sitting. By now, even their handwriting looks similar. But my mother smiles at my father in a polite way, a smile she reserves for strangers. I feel myself floating a little, sick, like the air has become gas, and I turn and flee down a long hallway.

I find Andrew, standing at a wide bank of windows, looking out at the mountains, which glow red-hot along the peaks from the last of the sun. I hand him the bag of presents and he takes it willingly, holds it like a briefcase.
'You know what?' he says, 'A woman just

went by and kicked me.' People stream past us, murmuring in German, Italian, men wheeling luggage dollies, children in their best winter clothes.

'I think it was on purpose, too,' he says. I tell Andrew I think that woman kicks people for a living, and that she seems to especially like kicking young men. Andrew is gangly and tall, his hands and elbows grown wide, his face solemn, thoughtful. He nudges me, and points her out in the crowd. She's a sight; a strange over-stuffed creature in a grey fur, wandering amongst the party dresses and overcoats and steamer trunks and huge potted trees. We observe her as she navigates the lobby, passing by several skiers, a desk clerk – all young men. She does nothing to them. We follow her progress until she disappears down one of the low dark hallways. Andrew looks at me in dismay, the bag of gifts dangling.

'What did I do?'

* * *

There's a phone call in the middle of the night. My grandparents are fighting – they're in Nevada.

Bishop and my dad hand the phone back and forth like a hot potato and hiss at each other:

'No way, I do this too often!'

'Well, don't look at me!'

'Take the damn phone!'

'I need a drink,' Castor says. We're all standing in the hallway outside my father's room in our pyjamas, everyone's hair in a wild mess and pillow marks on our faces. Poor Merry is trying her best to melt into a corner; her pyjamas are like kitchen curtains, frilly and see-through, and Andrew is in shock at the sight.

Bishop is speaking to my grandmother, holding the phone in a death-grip.

'No, don't! Mother, don't put him on! ... Hello, Father.'

'I need a drink!' Castor says.

'Of course you are, Father. No, just because you're seventy doesn't mean you're dead, *however* ... you ... how much?'

'Oh God!' says Castor.

'... in *two hours*?'

'It must be those bastards again,' Castor says.

'Nooo!' my mother trills with enjoyment, '*not* the famous Moe and Joe?'

'Who's Moe and Joe?' Andrew asks.

'Don't,' Dad says to Mum, 'don't you laugh.' She turns away and fiddles with the belt of her housecoat, her shoulders jiggling.

Bishop is squirming, now. I can hear my grandfather's tiny voice from the receiver. He's telling Bishop that he loves him, and Bishop is wincing, swearing silently. I strain to hear the small, thin sounds coming from the receiver, try to picture my grandparents in a desert casino: the lights and mirrors, the spill of change overflowing cups and pouring to the floor, and outside, the cars cruising past the splendid marquees, their tops folded down, rolling through soft desert air.

Castor gives up on finding a drink, and snatches the phone away from Bishop.

'Father, listen to me! Just tell them no and go get your ... What? I know you love Mother.'

'Who are Moe and Joe?' Merry whispers.

'And I love you too, Father.'

'Jesus!' says Bishop. By now, I'm wide awake. I badly want to get on the phone with my

grandfather, maybe get him to tell me he loves
me too. I wonder what it would feel like.

Castor puts his hand over the receiver and
hisses, 'They've got his car!' Dad flops down on
the unmade bed, his hands between his knees.

'Again?'

'Oh, sure,' says Bishop, 'he tells *you* about the
car, but does he mention it to me?'

Finally, Netty strides across the carpet and
takes the phone.

'Gerald?' she says, 'this is Netty speaking,' and
her voice is like a silk handkerchief floating down
through the air.

'Gerald!' she says, 'try to concentrate!'

When it's over, I gather, my grandfather has
agreed that he's an ass. Netty holds some kind of
power over him and she's single-handedly trussed
him up in a kind of invisible straitjacket, made
him promise to go home quietly. After that Dad
and his brothers go in search of a bottle, and the
rest of us file back to our rooms.

I lie awake and gaze at my mother – she's
smiling even in her sleep – and I try to picture
Dad and Mum together among the twinkling
lights, rolling some dice. I puzzle for a while over
whether it's hot in Nevada. With my father and
his maps and charts, I probably should know, but
I don't. I try to picture my parents, but after a
while the image erodes and I see, instead, my
father alone in Vegas, with his pockets turned
inside out. I turn over, then, turn my mind to
other things, like, if the hotel we're in has ghosts;
if they are angry; if they died while in love, or if
they died in pain; or if they, too, had wanted to
gamble and no one would let them. I wonder

. . . .

what kind of ghost my grandfather will make,
because it's obvious – he'll be one for sure; I
wonder what kind of ghost I might be.

* * *

It's the next morning, Christmas Eve, and my
mother comes into my room, puts a cup of coffee
on my dresser and sits down on the bed with me.

'How long have you been up?' I ask, grabbing
the coffee.

'Funeral time,' she says, 'thanks to your
father.' I struggle up, ready to defend my father
like a complete fool, but Netty is standing in the
doorway with Auntie Merry. Merry looks a little
haggard, trapped here with all of us. She tugs at
her sleeves and pats her shirt down. Netty looks
me over, takes in the tie-dyed T-shirt I use as a
nightie.

'Did your father buy you that?' she asks. I pull
the sheets up.

'No,' I say, insulted, 'I bought it with my own
money.'

'Oh good,' says Netty, 'I thought maybe he'd
lost his mind.'

All the women, me included, take the elevator
down. My brother is in the lobby, sitting behind
the front desk. His hair is still unbrushed,
standing up like flames. He and the two clerks
look up as I approach.

'Their root directory is screwed,' Andrew says,
and the man beams and pats Andrew on the back,
enthuses in Italian.

No one knows where Andrew got it, but he
can walk up to any machine and fix it. He has
never been seen reading a computer magazine,
and yet he knows what's current, what's defunct,

The Funeral

he knows machine languages. He puts a finger on
a squiggle in a senseless wall of squiggles and
says: 'That should be zero there, not one.' The
same holds true for more primitive machines:
toasters, furnaces, cars. He bends over the oily
mass of pipes and hoses in my father's car,
grimaces, points at an unidentified steel lump.
'You bought it used?'

After breakfast we find out some of the truth.
My father explains it in detail while my mother
squirms and sighs and stares at me as if I am
responsible. It seems that asking: 'Who died?',
especially when language is a barrier, is unwise.
Castor had been told about a family who perished
in a fire, down in the city, nearly a year ago.
Merry thought it was one of us, someone she
hadn't met yet. Bishop thought he'd found a man
with a missing child, but it turned out the man
was just showing him baby photos.

In fact, the man who had died was Otto, the
organist at the church situated directly across
from the hotel. He was eighty-seven years old,
had had dozens of children from several mothers,
and he ate dinner and drank every night of his life
in the hotel. He was a fixture, a local character,
and now he was dead, and we were all invited to
his funeral.

Andrew and I descend the hill, following the
road into town, our cheeks numb and our fingers
screaming in our pockets because we made the
mistake of whipping snowballs at tour buses and
parked cars until the cold got us. I like it when
my brother lets me hang around, but still, I'm
thinking about last night, feeling sorry for old
men who can't do what they want anymore.

'Do you think Grandad is crazy?' I ask
Andrew.

'Yes,' he says.

'How can you be sure?' I ask.

This worries me. I've been troubled by the
suspicion that I'll end up like him – gambling,
scaring the crap out of strangers, telling
ridiculous stories enough times that I start
believing them myself. For instance, I'm afraid to
get my driver's licence. My grandfather was law-
abiding at first, and then, one day, he parked right
on the sidewalk, a boulevard of broken saplings
behind him. It's been that way ever since.

'Oh, he's crazy all right,' says Andrew,
warming to the subject 'but Grandad was
probably normal once, like you or me.'

'Oh, no.'

'I blame old age, I blame TV. You know, before
TV, people had much higher IQ's?'

'But, what if ...'

'It's true. A dog has as much IQ as a four-year-
old human. Depending on the breed. And
scientists think that some brain diseases come
from too much ...'

The idea horrifies me. If it happened to
Grandfather, it might happen to me. My worst
fear would come true; I might not be me, after all.
I might be someone else, someone really
unpleasant, just waiting to pop open and spray all
over the place, like a bad can of pop. I'll be old
and crazy and never get a date. I'll be paranoid.
Broke. Write abusive letters to the Queen. I'll
never leave my house, squint through the drapes
when the mailman steps on my porch. I'll stand
over a boiling pot of water and hear messages

about all the bad things Danny Kaye is saying
about me. It's horrible. I look to Andrew, my
brother, for help and only then realize that he's
been trying to get my attention.

'*Look,*' he says and points my head with his
hands, and I see the white rump of a deer walking
lazily into the darkness of the trees. It turns its
white tail away, blends in, and disappears. We
walk on into town then, Andrew telling me I
zone out way too much these days.

The man behind the desk is smiling at guests
with his nice white teeth. It's a dull, businesslike
smile, but when he drops it he looks nasty,
devious, interesting. He's twice my age, but I sit
down on a plush sofa and consider him anyway.
He's probably married. I am drowning in my own
family – not that I resent it. I just have no
privacy, no room to manoeuvre. I have an
overwhelming urge to go over to the desk and be
frank with that man, watch his face fall, watch
those white teeth stop smiling. Maybe he'd turn
me down. Maybe he wouldn't. Instead, I pace
around the halls.

I enter a dim hallway, stare up at the beards of
moose, the strange plastic noses of deer, tongues
stuck out a little, as if bleating. I am deep into a fit
of the creeps when I remember Andrew's words
about dogs being as smart as children. How smart
are deer? I look at a mounted head and decide: not
smart enough. What a horrible way to end up;
wood and sawdust inside your skin, holding
plastic nose and eyes in place. A woman ambles
by me, humming. People are milling about the
lobby, huge heads lolling over them, and no one
minds. Just me. I figure I'd better go lie down.

My mother and Aunt Netty are getting hysterical in the hallway. I can't hear the subject, but I can guess. In my mind, my father and Castor are getting smaller and smaller and their clothes are billowing around them. They wave their arms for help. Merry is out there with them, but she is silent except for a little 'Oh, my' or 'I see'. She sounds alarmed. I've been eating the candy my brother and I bought down in town – marzipan frogs, angels and flowers. Salty licorice. Squat, frilly chocolate tarts. I can actually feel myself getting fatter. I'm trying to read Castor's magazine about the high aristocracy, but it's in French and a very fussy kind of French. If I am reading correctly, this prince in the Netherlands has been to the moon and back and now he wants to plant corn. Between this and the voices from next door, I am wishing I was somewhere else.

* * *

The entire hotel is invited to the funeral and we all shuffle into the church to rousing organ music and laughter and the sound of dogs howling everywhere outside. Andrew leans over:

'If the organist is dead, then who's playing the organ?'

During the funeral service, my father sits at one end of the pew and my mother sits at the other. The rest of the family is wedged between them. Trying not to doze, I watch a man's smooth leather toe rise and fall gently in the quiet cavern of the church, as if the man is hearing music in his head. I fight the horrible wooze of sleepiness while the rector delivers the eulogy.

Otto, he says, was a good, kind, decent person, a man who gave such love to his children that he

. . . .

was wealthy in his soul as a result. He was generous to his friends, and generous to the world, since he gave the gift of music. My mother sniffles and takes my hand. There are a few quotes from the Bible about music and God's breath. I can smell Christmas dinner cooking across the street at the hotel. Dogs whine and scratch at the closed chapel door.

Two very old men are seated in front of my mother and me. One leans over and tells the other in a hoarse, stage whisper: 'We must be at the wrong funeral.'

'Should have worn ear plugs,' hisses the other.

The rector, who is new, never met Otto, the man he is eulogizing. By the end of the service, the pews are boiling with unrest. This was Otto, finally falling dead in the pine grove, reeking of liquor, eighty-seven years old and halfway home. Otto, who threw things, who harried local girls and terrorized his many children, who badgered money out of people and never paid it back. Otto, tossing a cigarette down a bartender's blouse. Otto, drinking in church, the floor around his organist's bench foul with phlegm. Otto, called 'the nickel man' by children in town.

At the reception afterwards, we all huddle like cattle in case someone should ask us what we are doing there, or in what way we knew the deceased. One by one we check our watches while the aroma of turkey and beef and steaming vegetables vexes and distracts us.

'Well,' says Merry finally, in a tiny voice, 'I don't think Otto would mind if we had dinner now, do you?'

* * *

. . . .

We have all discovered, to our secret pleasure, that Merry is a glutton. She is furious and impatient, trying now to ignite the plum pudding with her plastic lighter, but it just won't start. She had wanted to give up and eat it unlit, but was vetoed. Netty keeps pouring rum over the pudding, so that by now it's sitting in a puddle half an inch deep. My mother is sitting beside me with her napkin at the ready in case anyone singes their eyebrows off. As usual when Castor is around, the noise in the room is almost unbearable. It's lucky we've got a little room to ourselves.

A beautiful waiter wanders around behind our chairs, making helpful suggestions to Merry, tripping on wrapped presents and generally being a distraction. He has the outrageous name of Felton, he speaks English, and he has no idea how to kiss. His breath, I have discovered, tastes like cherries. I am gazing at his long face in the wavering glow of candles and the dim overhead light. He winks at me and my mother catches him; Felton turns red, grasps a few empty glasses and rushes from the room.

'His name is Felton,' I tell my mother, and she fixes me with an appraising look.

She's starting to catch on about me.

I take another drink of wine, sigh, wonder when we are going to open presents. For the last few minutes my father has been kicking me lightly, trying to find a comfortable position in which to sleep, and it looks like he's found one. I am always stunned at the way my father sleeps. Castor is laughing derisively at Bishop.

· ·

'What a crock!' he bellows, 'I suppose you believe in the Loch Ness monster.'

'Look, it's absolutely true!' Bishop is grinning.

'... and UFO's and ghosts. I suppose you pray, too. Does he pray, Merry?'

'Oh, you swine,' says Bishop. Merry looks up from the alcoholic lump before her, lighter still hissing in her hand.

'What's so funny about praying?' She's saying it as much to Bishop as to Castor.

'Ignore him, dear,' Netty says, 'he's running his mouth.'

We must be the worst guests in the hotel, which is probably why we have our own little room to eat in. Still, I'm feeling all right about the world. I've had more wine than I'm used to and everything seems gracious and happy and secure for once. I look at my mother, who I miss a lot sometimes, and at Andrew, whose body seems to change every week, and for a moment I wish we could all stay like this. I think: wouldn't it be nice if we all died suddenly, without hurting, without knowing anything had happened, and went on as ghosts, having dinner and arguing and never growing old? What would be wrong with that? I wonder about my grandparents, old and wild as they are, without the first thought in their minds about mortality. And I wonder if Otto is anywhere around here, drifting through the halls, pissed off, invisible, throwing things at tourists.

I'm thinking about that, thinking about all of us, and the afterlife, and how maybe I could take the waiter with us, when, without any particular reason or warning, the pudding bangs on like a blow torch. Blue flames leap at the light fixture

overhead; chairs are shoved back in alarm,
barking against the floor; Merry and Castor both
scream.

One minute the room is noisy, the next, it's
thunderous. Poor Andrew wakes with a jolt,
blithering and confused.
    'Substitute real oranges,' he says.
    The flames streak upward, and the air is filled
with the aroma of hot butter, currants, and failing
fireproof ceiling tiles. It's an emergency; my
mother, with her napkin held up in absurd
defence, Castor with both hands pressed to his
mouth, roaring through his fingers, my father
rising unwilling from sleep, smacking his lips,
one serene eye open and unfocused on the blaze.
It's fantastic, brilliant. I know it then, this is the
moment I've been waiting for: this is us, a picture
of us, my whole family caught mid-sentence,
mid-gesture, light pouring out, momentarily
bright as a flash.

Acknowledgements

'Heaven Is a Place That Starts with H' appeared in What! magazine #27, 1991, and was reprinted in the anthology *Best Canadian Stories, 1992*.

'Fear Itself' appeared in very different form in This Magazine, Vol. 24, #5, December 1991.

'Help Me, Jacques Cousteau' appeared in CKLN's Programme Guide, October 1993, and in a slightly different form in *This Magazine*, vol. 27, #8, April 1994.

'The Lakemba' appeared, in very different form, in a chapbook of the same name, from Contra Mundo Press, 1990.

This is a work of fiction. Any resemblance to persons living or dead is not only coincidental, but is also a damned lie, according to my mother.

I would like to thank the taxpayers of Ontario for their support through the Ontario Arts Council and the Toronto Arts Council.

I would also like to thank the lovely Jean Yoon,

. . . .

Stuart Ross, and my parents (all of 'em) for
understanding the vagaries of fiction, Andrew for
being himself in more ways than one, Clint
Burnham, Victor Coleman, Katy Chan, Maggie
Helwig, David Demchuck, the People of the
Republic of Rathnelly and the kind people at the
Banff Centre, also Barbara Gowdy for her support,
and warm thanks to Steven Heighton for setting
it all in motion.

Special thanks to Kevin Connolly, writer, editor
and *bon vivant*, apple o' my eye.

Heartfelt thanks to John Metcalf for his
enthusiasm, gentle editing, patience and
motivation.

About the Author

ADRIAN ADAMSON

Gil Adamson was born and raised in Toronto. She studied Philosophy and Anthropology at the University of Toronto and continues to live in Toronto. Her fiction has been featured in *Quarry, Paragraph, This Magazine, Rampike* and *Best Canadian Stories*.